The Changing Quest

C.A. Powell

To Colin, hope you enjoy from Cor.

Double Dragon Publishing

The Changing Quest
Copyright © 2006 C.A. Powell

Double Dragon Press

Published by
Double Dragon Publishing, Inc.
PO Box 54016
1-5762 Highway 7 East
Markham, Ontario L3P 7Y4 Canada
http://www.double-dragon-ebooks.com
http://www.double-dragon-publishing.com

ISBN: 1-55404-325-5

A DDP First Edition February 24, 2006
Book Layout and
Cover Art by Deron Douglas

PREFACE

In the year 560 A.D., King Ceawlin took the throne of West Saxon Land with the unstinting help of his younger brother, Cutha. Together, they had ruled with a firm hand for seven years, and successfully resisted continuing external threats.

To the east lay the kingdom of Kent, ruled by King Ethelbert, who was always poised to launch his Jutish army into the West Saxons' domain. The northern borders were menaced by the Angles of Mercia, while in Dumnonia, to the west, the Celts held nothing but hatred for the Saxon colonisers. Indeed, much of Ceawlin's kingdom had been won from Dumnonia by earlier West Saxon kings.

There were no links of any kind between West Saxon Land and Dumnonia, whose cultures, races and language were completely different. Border skirmishes and small raids were commonplace, though they had never developed into full-scale war.

The Dumnonian King had great respect for Ceawlin, who was already, after only seven years as a monarch, being referred to as Bretwalda, King of Britain. Ceawlin, for his part, had no desire to create trouble with Dumnonia, when the borders with Kent and Mercia held so many problems for him.

The Dumnonian raids were mainly against a group of separatist-minded Saxons known as the Gewisse, who occupied settlements along the border. Being kept busy by the enemy raids, the Gewisse thus had little time to protest against West Saxon overlordship.

The Gewisse, one of many Saxon races within West Saxon Land, were different in that their ancestors had started colonising the area a generation before the rest of the West Saxons.

The remainder of Ceawlin's subjects saw them as a threat to the stability of the kingdom with their separatist attitudes, and viewed the continuous skirmishing with the Dumnonians as, at least, a way of preventing internal troubles. However, the Gewisse argued they were losing their identity because of their absorption into West Saxon Land.

In early September of 567, separatist views had become inflamed to such an extent, they were prepared to disregard the commands of Caewlin. Dumnonia's king had died, leaving the title to be fought for among the nobility, thus causing the kingdom to break up. Hearing of this, the Gewisse decided to take advantage of the situation by invading.

Ceawlin was greatly tempted to agree with them for the overall gain of his kingdom; but the danger of Mercia and Kent attacking when his back was turned forced him to forbid any expeditions into Dumnonia. Resentment among the Gewisse was so deep, they decided to disobey him and try to win a separate kingdom for themselves in Dumnonia.

They were supported in this by their anti-Christian priesthood, who had good reason to dislike Dumnonia because of the successful influence the Christian religion was beginning to have upon the Saxons, Angles and Jutes.

Christian missionaries were coming into the Teutonic areas of Britain from countries like Hibernia, Cymru and Dumnonia in order to try and convert the pagan colonists. Gods like Woden, Thunder, Ty and Frigg were losing their influence upon the Germanic nobility.

Ceawlin would certainly not allow the West Saxon priesthood to intimidate his position, even though he himself paid no attention to the Christian missionaries.

The proposed attack on Dumnonia offered a chance for the pagan priesthood to hit back at Christianity and they used all their power to encourage the separatists to invade Dumnonia—although the Gewisse saw no need for the blessing of their priests in the venture. Their acceptance of the priests' support was based on the fact it would profit them a little among the people of West Saxon Land, for despite the general lack of enthusiasm for the religion, no

Saxon would openly condemn the gods. Fear and suspicion of the unknown could still be aroused.

Early September saw the Gewisse recklessly and blindly leave their crops in order to battle Dumnonia. These 'farmers-turned-warriors' believed it necessary to abandon their harvest in order to prepare for the coming campaign, sure that a quick victory within Dumnonia's eastern territory would bring wealth in the form of plunder and a large Celtic harvest—and land to settle on.

Three armies were to invade Dumnonia, each led by an overlord chosen from the most wealthy Gewisse chieftains.

Each army was made up of small clans led by land-owning sub-chieftains, who virtually owned all the men in their settlements. All would strike out for the west: along the northern coast, Fulcher would lead eight thousand men, while Egbert's seven thousand travelled the southern coast. Taking the mid-country route would be Arfast, with three thousand men.

CHAPTER ONE

A morning chill gave warning of the summer's dying days, while the bleak, overcast sky threatened to drop its wet load upon the Saxon meadows and the settlement standing desolately among them.

The solitary Gewisse hamlet sat in the middle of a stockade and within the wooded walls, the rectangular huts had a shabby and tired look. The dirty, mud-encrusted thatched roofs looked in urgent need of attention before winter set in. A knowing eye would deduce that the inhabitants were used to a very modest living compared with most West Saxon communities and that it was rather late in the morning for such folk to be sleeping. However, the previous night had been spent celebrating and all nursed hangovers—women and children not excluded.

The forthcoming invasion, due to commence that afternoon, was the reason for the revelry. It would have been wiser to set off during the early hours of the morning, but no self-respecting Gewisse Saxon would let anything stand in the way of an excuse to make merry.

Leofstan, the community's chieftain, was thirty-nine and his abode was easily distinguished from the rest—being slightly bigger with a fine wooden door decorated with carvings of Germanic gods. This same door suddenly swung open violently, smashing against the hut's wall, and framed in the doorway was the stout, bedraggled form of Leofstan. He staggered out into the dusty yard towards the well, cursing and kicking at two hens that got in his way.

"Go on, shoo! You pesky things," he spat in a huff.

The bird's shrill protestations filled the morning air as they flapped their wings and scurried off in panic, scattered feathers descending to settle upon the ground in their vacated wake.

As he reached the well, Leofstan frowned in perplexity as his vision settled upon the settlement's cockerel, which was lying dead in the dust.

"What in Woden's..." he muttered, then gave up on the sentence.

Quickly, he pulled up the wooden bucket and stuck his head in the cold water, the shock of which immediately brought him to his senses with a jolt.

"Phew!" He shivered spasmodically.

Bringing his head out of the bucket, he shook his matted, wet hair, sprinkling water all around on the dry sod. Then suddenly, he remembered he had already got up once that morning, before the dawn.

He picked up the limp body of the cockerel and muttered to himself.

"Stupid cockerel—fancy cock-a-doodle-doing at the crack of dawn on a morning when I have a head as thick as an oak tree. Oh, the Gods! You lousy, stupid bird."

Nonchalantly tossing the dead cockerel away, he looked around to see if any other person, beside himself, was up. There was no one, and upon taking a deep breath, he knew the worst effects of his hangover were gone. With a malicious smile creasing his face, he began to bellow.

"Morning is here and almost over! Come on, you lazy goats, get up now." He paused and heard the sounds of stirring in the huts all around. "Come on," he roared again, "what are you waiting for—winter?"

A door opened behind him and a thin, fair-haired youth with soft, fine orange whiskers emerged scratching his unkempt, greasy locks.

"Is your father up yet, Cuthbert?" questioned Leofstan sternly.

"Yes, my Lord, he is getting dressed." The youth was squinting rapidly as though not sure whether he was awake or still dreaming.

"Good, pull yourself together now and listen. I want you to go into the hills and tell that estranged nephew of mine to get his estranged backside down here quickly, or we shall leave without him. You can take one of my horses, any of them, except Flash. Is that understood?"

"Yes, my Lord, very clear," replied Cuthbert with signs of enthusiasm as he hurried off, for the chore was a pleasant one. A chance to ride a horse and visit Sighelme, Leofstan's nephew, was always cherished among the community's youths.

All around the fort, people were waking and the women began walking to the compost heap just outside the stockade with their buckets, chattering together as they disposed of the night's waste.

Leofstan walked about the settlement, which was suddenly teeming with life, calling for the rest of the men to get up. Another youth with long, oily fair hair staggered out before him.

"Get everyone up, Edgar," he demanded. "Tell them I want all the men to come to me in the hall."

"Yes, my Lord," replied Edgar, jumping to the task. He ran off calling, "All men to the hall. All men to the hall."

Leofstan immediately made his way to the place, which was by far, the largest of all the settlement's buildings—bigger even than the barn. Rectangular in shape like the huts, and with a slanting thatched roof, it could seat all the community's inhabitants quite comfortably and was used for banquets and debates.

The burly chieftain sighed as he entered, for the place was littered with the remains of the previous night's celebrations. Benches were overturned and drinking horns, clay mugs and wooden plates lay strewn on the floor among bones and half-eaten vegetables.

"The women will have to start clearing up the mess after we leave to join Arfast for the attack on Dumnonia," he muttered to himself. Arching his aching back and rubbing the back of his neck, he strode awkwardly through the debris, pushing one of the benches out of the way with his foot as he made his way to the single high chair at the end of the hall, where he sat himself down.

Cuthbert's father, Hubert, and another community elder called Lambert, stood in silhouette at the doorway.

"The aftermath is always a little depressing, Leofstan," said Hubert, yanking a large toothed comb through his long, graying hair and stroking his beard to a point. He did not address the chieftain as 'Lord'— none of the elders did. It was an unofficial custom for the two senior elders of the community to address Leofstan by name, as they had before he had taken over the chieftainship from his father. Other members of the community addressed him as Lord, except for Sighelme, to whom he was known as uncle, and Aldred, his absent son, who called him father.

"Yes, it does dampen the spirit holding council in this mess. I feel as though I would be more dignified sitting on top of the compost heap," replied Leofstan, frowning at the sight of Lambert, who looked very haggard with the night's aftereffects.

The wretched man greeted him and walked over to one of the benches, turned it upright and sat down. Resting his elbows on his knees with his forehead in his cupped hands, he allowed his bedraggled light brown hair to fall, masking his face.

"Oh, Woden, I really do need all this on the very day we are to go to battle against these Celtic Dumnonians." He took a deep breath and blew out.

Leofstan smiled wickedly. "Seeing and hearing him," he said, looking at Hubert while jerking his head in the direction of Lambert, "makes me feel so much better." With a deep belly laugh, he got up out of his seat and walked over to the door, saying, "Those youngsters are not a patch on us old ones; we are always the first to be ready."

Lambert's face suddenly protruded through his dangling locks to look up at Hubert exchanging a grin and a wink. Both men knew Leofstan's mood got better if he saw other people around him were slower, or in a worse state of health than he was. Sometimes, it was better to treat the old chieftain with especial care when he had been drinking large quantities of ale the night before.

"Come on, you youngsters!" shouted Leofstan, who was beginning to feel exceptionally pleased with himself.

All the young men of the settlement appeared at once from behind one of the huts, where Hubert and Lambert had told them to wait. They, too, knew Leofstan was in his element if he could find some examples of youthful slovenliness to make fun of.

Lambert grinned, then whispered to Hubert, "The old boy would be livid if he had any idea how his community whimsically plots behind his back to indulge him and make him happy—allowing him to look superior all the time."

Hubert smirked and held his finger to his lip. "Shoosh! Not now, Lambert," he whispered. "He'll hear you for sure."

"Why this very morning we've all waited indoors until our Lord emerged, just so he would feel he can ride the aftereffects of drinking better than the rest of us—and so he might take pleasure in pointing it out, too."

"An indulgence for our Lord," added Hubert. It was the elder's custom also, to call Leofstan 'Lord' behind his back.

The community was not disrespectful for they all loved him greatly, though he was erratic at times.

Soon, the unwittingly indulged chieftain was feeling exceptionally jovial and he walked back into the hall with three youths following him. Edgar, son of Lambert, was one of them, while the other two were brothers named Turnstan and Rhinehold.

Seating himself in his high chair again, Leofstan began to address them about the campaign against the Dumnonians.

"Well, I hope everyone has packed everything he needs." His significant look at the three youngsters brought uncertain words in return, and he went on, "We are just waiting for Cuthbert to return with Sighelme—then we shall leave here to join Arfast's invasion force."

"What about Aldred, my Lord?" asked Turnstan.

Leofstan took a deep breath and sighed. "Aldred, the eldest of my three sons and one daughter and the only one of my offspring touching the age of manhood, is away visiting the daughter of a neighbouring chieftain, to whom he is betrothed, as you all know. It is an unfortunate thing that he was absent when this adventure was planned. I am afraid we must leave without him. If we wait for him to return, we shall miss the border crossing and have to catch up with Arfast well inside Dumnonia. We could miss a major battle, and then other villages would say we arrived when most of the fighting was over. You know how folk talk. Aldred, I'm sure, will be quite capable of catching us up, and besides, he may even go along with his future father-in-law, who will be riding under Egbert to the south."

There were a few more minor questions, all of which were answered. Leofstan then dismissed the youngsters so he could talk privately with Hubert and Lambert.

The three young warriors walked out of the hall towards the well, clearly disappointed Leofstan's eldest son, Aldred, was not with them.

"He'll be displeased he missed out on this venture," said Edgar.

"If I know Aldred, he'll be riding like the wind to be with us," added Rhinehold.

Turnstan nodded his approval. "For once, brother, I agree with you."

"Oh may the sign of such wonders be a taste of what is to come," reproached Rhinehold tartly as it was the brothers' lot in life to constantly bicker, much to the amusement of others.

"Aww, them two are off again," called one of the women of the group that was gathering by the well.

The three young men swaggered over to chat and show off in their cocky and youthful way among the mothers, sisters and all the children, who seemed to be more than usually active, while they waited for the men to leave.

Again, the women began to flirt with the young lads. "Got lots of swagger, you young boys," giggled one.

All three complied and began to show off, holding out their spatha swords and unsheathing their scramasaxes—the long single-edged knives of the Saxons.

"Is that your weapon, Edgar?" chuckled one of the elder women. "Aww, I bet you could do some damage with that." She looked at the married women who all laughed, while the younger unattached ones grinned and blushed with embarrassment.

"Easy, ladies," scolded Turnstan mockingly.

"Aww catch him," replied the elder woman again. "I bet he's got a glint in his blade."

More giggling followed, as it was a common thing for the elder married women often made sport of the young men in front of the younger girls. It was a way of bringing down barriers for the not too distant future.

The sound of hoofbeats, thundering towards the stockade entrance, drew their attention away from the light-hearted frolics as Cuthbert rode in, followed by Sighelme and a young squire, Wilfred, who was seated behind him.

After greeting Edgar, Turnstan, Rhinehold and Sighelme turned to Wilfred and gave him a reassuring word before dismounting. He then made his way to the hall where Leofstan was deep in discussion with Hubert and Lambert. He broke off to welcome his nephew.

"Greetings, Sighelme, I'm pleased you are so prompt."

"Greetings, Uncle," he replied, surveying the mess about him. "I would like to ask a great favour of you concerning Wilfred, my squire. I would like him to come with us as a warrior, so he may play his part in the fighting for the settlement."

"I know about your young squire," replied Leofstan after some consideration. " And I know of his eagerness to prove himself among us. This is a good thing and it must be encouraged. He may come if you wish, but there will be conditions, which I shall tell you about later."

Bowing his thanks, Sighelme left the elders and went back outside, where Wilfred was still seated on the horse waiting apprehensively in case he might be refused permission to accompany the invasion.

"The answer is yes," Sighelme smiled broadly, "but my uncle is going to impose conditions. What they are yet—I cannot say."

Beaming delightedly, Wilfred leapt from the horse as Edgar, Cuthbert, Turnstan and Rhinehold congratulated him on his new honorary status as a warrior.

"Well done, Wilfred," added one of the women, while others nodded and smiled approvingly.

There was little time for further conversation as Leofstan, with the two elders, came out and began to mount up. With farewells, they made ready to leave; four on horseback, including Sighelme, while the rest were on foot.

"Right then!" Leofstan yelled, while holding a clenched fist above his head. "Let us be gone from here."

All the women and children ran out of the stockade to give their menfolk a rapturous send off.

CHAPTER TWO

From out of the west came the blustering wind, which tore across the Dumnonian moorlands like an invisible entity—a maternal derangement of unknowing apprehension—that swished about in panic amid a long line of decrepit, weatherworn refugees who were battling the marshy slopes despairingly. Thin-faced Celtic peasant men screamed and cursed as cartwheels sank into the mud, while their women tried to console the infants. The old and sick managed as best they could, some riding forlornly in the carts, others more hard-pressed on foot. Their tattered garments gave little protection against the panic-stricken wind and dampness of the moors. Heavy coughs tore out among the refugees— racking the undernourished bodies of the disheartened people.

The shredded draughts rose in scattered blusters to unite into one all being howling wind. Moving across an overcast sky, wailing like a tremendous animal that had received a mortal blow, it descended with new curiosity towards a small deserted Celtic village that stood in the middle of unharvested wheatfields. Like a giant godly hand, the wind stroked across and around the meadows and three dirt tracks that cut through the field towards the abandoned village. One path came in from a southeasterly direction and another from the north, but a freshly trampled one led west into the moors. It swished about the circular stone huts with their thatched roofs that rose to form a cone and the discarded debris that littered the muddy ground. Scraps of fur still hung from smashed frames, and the remains of a broken loom blocked the doorway of a hut. A mangy dog sniffed amid the rubble—the only living creature in the deserted settlement.

Frustration now took a firm grip on the wind and its small draughty legions invaded doorways. Fingerlike air pockets churned the dust, but found no pungent smells of plague or sickness.

The dog looked up fearfully as the ghostly whines intensified and yelped once before running off into the fields, leaving the inquisitive wind to its eastward journey. Again, it rose into the fretful sky and the weird cries from the nooks and crannies ceased their demanding shrills, allowing the dust to settle while the broken loom stopped its creaking.

Ranging over farmland, hills and forests, the wind continued to search for the reason why these people were leaving their homes and unharvested fields.

There was no disease in any of the villages, and no blight on the abandoned crops.

Eastward it surged until it came across the scattered hordes of men, barbarian men—pagans from the conquered eastern side of the island. These men were foreign to the land and uninvited. All were fiercely armed for battle as they travelled deeper into the west.

"Invaders," was the word the wind had sought; that was why the Dumnonian people were hastily leaving their homes and why their great and respected kingdom had fallen into decline. Bewildered by the political turmoil that gripped the land after the death of the king, the people had become like frightened sheep, running in vain to the furthest corner of their field in search of protection.

All the villages in the path of the invading forces were deserted, void of any movement. The only resistance had been in the odd stronghold owned by men of high regard in Dumnonian society who were too proud to run; whose servants were too loyal to desert.

Desolate, the wind no longer violently swept the land. It had travelled far and learnt much and as each new truth was discovered, it had slowed, as if to mourn. It descended and gently swept the smoldering ruins of a recently razed settlement, whose former inhabitants lay scattered in the dust, having been savagely mutilated.

For ages unrecorded in man's history, the west wind had journeyed across this land. At no other time, before or after, would it feel such grief as for the period when this Christian land of Britons fell under the onslaught of the pagan English tribes: a time in Europe's history that was to become known to men as the 'Dark Ages'.

The wind held its torment within as it avoided the approaching horseman. He was from the east. A Saxon warrior and one of high esteem for he was richly dressed. The warrior's right hand clenched the hilt of his spatha, which hung from his left hip in a brown leather and bronze framed scabbard—the long two-edged sword was the preferred weapon of his people. Gently, he released his grip and let his hand dangle to his right beside the long single-edged scramasax knife. His long fair hair hung down upon his round, concave shield, which was fastened upon his back. Along the shield's circumference, a strong strip of metal kept the edge intact and at each quarter, four extra strips of metal led to the centre, which was strengthened by a huge boss.

The wind swept slowly over the corpses, as though gathering their humiliated souls and bearing them safely over the lone horseman's head, almost as if wishing in no way to come in contact with him.

The warrior halted his mount in respect. Conscious of the soul-bearing wind, he convinced himself the Valkyrie war goddesses were riding with it. After the brief pause, the Saxon proceeded towards the fallen stronghold, through the wreckage and carnage, the death and destruction that had been wrought upon these people. He was captured by the sight—not with shame, nor with pride, but with a curious fascination. He had never seen so many dead people before and was held by the spectacle before him.

With arrogant grace, the young warrior dismounted and began to walk among the dead, surveying all about him. A broken spearhead caught his attention, the only visible remnant of any form of weaponry amid the debris.

Squatting on his haunches, he studied the spearhead, which he could tell at a glance was Saxon. "In what manner were you forged?" he whispered to the object as though it were sentient and believed in some curious way, it communicated with him. The maker of the weapon was a well-known blacksmith from a neighbouring community called Osbert. This, he could tell at a glance.

The young man smiled in satisfaction, saying: "Well, Osbert, Aldred is catching up with the rest of the lads."

The white stallion snorted and Aldred stood looking once more upon the turmoil of destruction.

It was the smell of death that was making the horse unsteady and he walked torwards the beast as a violent gust of wind whipped his long fair hair across his face. In a nearby derelict hut, a clay pot was blown from a shelf and smashed on the floor. The stallion reared as he approached. One hand went to the reins, whilst the other grasped the hilt of his sword once again.

After making a quick survey in the direction of the hut, Aldred mounted his nervous steed. "Yes," he said, stroking his horse's mane reassuringly. "There is anger in the wind—much anger."

The pull and kick to direct the horse were unnecessary as the white beast seemed as eager as its rider to leave the ruins and reach their goal. Travelling without a cloak, Aldred did not relish a night alone without the warmth of a campfire, or the comfort of friendly company in the Dumnonian wilderness.

As dusk approached, Aldred saw the campfires in the distance and his spirits rose as he rode his mount towards them. The smell of the fires was carried on, what was now, a gentle breeze under the star-filled sky.

Passing the sentries, he dismounted and began searching for familiar faces. His heart lifted when he saw his cousin hurrying across the camp carrying a bundle of firewood.

"Sighelme," he called excitedly.

The youth stopped upon hearing his name and tried to make out who was calling him from beyond the campfire. For a moment, the blaze dazzled him. Then recognition came and, with a large smile. "Aldred," he yelled happily. "You got here at last. Your father's unrest is at an end."

"Is it, indeed?" said Aldred mockingly. "Mine is newly aroused."

With an understanding smile, he replied, "Don't judge him too harshly, Aldred," knowing he would never do such a thing, "how could he hold his men up until you came home from your lady's camp?" Aldred responded to Sighelme's teasing with a playful clump on the head.

Together, they walked deeper into the camp, Sighelme clutching the mass of twigs and bramble in his arms, Aldred still leading his horse.

Sighelme's height and unfashionable dress made him very noticeable. His hair was shorter than most, less than shoulder length, but still very untidy. Matted lumps of ginger hair protruded defiantly from his scalp. His legs were also distinct, for he had suffered from rickets as a child and it had made them bow-shaped. His clothes were very tattered and there was an uncommon lack of jewellery about him. Despite his oddness, however, he had an agile air and moved gracefully through the camp on his spiderlike limbs.

Upon reaching the fire, Sighelme let out a jubilant yell, "Look who I've found!" Excited shouts arose from the young men of his community, hands were outstretched to greet him and Aldred found himself enjoying the welcome hospitality of his friends. Happy to accept it, he then allowed his gaze to fall upon his father, Leofstan, who had remained seated and said nothing.

They stared at one another, neither speaking. All around, the men had suddenly fallen silent, the eyes of the young on Aldred and those of the older men on Leofstan.

Aldred's face creased slightly with a smile, then his father's did the same. A chuckle escaped from Aldred's throat and all at once, his father let loose with a roar of laughter. He jumped up and embraced his son warmly and very proudly.

"Welcome, Aldred," he shouted, holding up one of his son's arms for all within the light of the fire to see. This action was greeted with a great cheer of approval. "You have arrived in time to hear of Lord Fulcher's men, who are travelling to the north of us. This priest brings news from their camp." Leofstan pointed to a remorseful looking holy man, who was sitting with the rest of them.

Aldred and his father then seated themselves to listen to the priest and, on reading the look of sadness in his face, Aldred felt a shiver of concern.

Soon Sighelme, who had been attending to Aldred's horse, joined the party, and the priest began his story.

"It happened this evening, about four hours from sunset. Fulcher and some of the other noblemen rode off from the main body of his forces. They came to a stream, where they saw a beautiful young woman who ran into the woods on the opposite side as soon as she saw them. Foolishly, they decided to give chase and, when they were halfway across the stream, a massive hail of arrows rained down on them from a hidden enemy, sending the horses wild with confusion. A vicious charge followed next and it was during this that Fulcher fell."

The priest paused and allowed his gaze to fall into the fire, where orange tongues danced across the logs. Searching deep within its radiance, he was able to resume his sad tidings.

"Although Fulcher had fallen, his body was not lost to the river. His devoted men bore the smashed corpse to the shore, where they made a stand as our foes began to cut them down, one by one. However, one of our riders successfully rode the gauntlet and managed to get help from the main body of our men and a considerable force immediately set off to the rescue. The Dumnonians had withdrawn across the river and into the woods when the rescue party arrived, but we did manage to capture one of their lookouts."

He paused again, and an impatient murmur came from the captivated audience.

The priest looked at the inquisitive faces and, for the first time, he allowed a smile to cross his marble face. "Oh, yes," he replied to their unasked question, "yes, he spoke when we had finished with him. Apparently, there is a warrior from Cymru, a Gwentman called Caradoc, who has gathered a force with the aim of pushing us back to the east. Many of the people from these parts are joining him and he has won much of their confidence by staging highly successful attacks on small foraging parties and then vanishing into the moors." Here the priest stopped, as Leofstan stood up.

"This Caradoc could be a very dangerous man," said the chieftain after some contemplation. "Is there no way we can draw him out of his nest for an all-out battle?"

"Well, according to the captive, Caradoc is preparing to meet us in open conflict, when and where he thinks right," replied the priest.

Leofstan nodded thoughtfully and said, "So if we keep on advancing, sooner or later, Caradoc will stand against us?"

"Of that you can be assured, and soon, before we advance too deeply," added the priest.

Talk of Cardoc ended there, to lie dormant within every Saxon's mind until the time of battle.

The rest of the night was spent in telling Aldred of the fortifications they had stormed earlier that day, the smouldering remnants of which Aldred had passed through.

Aldred tried hard to listen to all the tales, but his fatigue began to overcome him and his body eagerly absorbed the fire's heat as sleep conquered his mind.

CHAPTER THREE

The Saxon army left at the first signs of daylight, leaving behind them sooted mounds with black, charred logs poking through the grey surface of their abandoned and dead campfires. From a distance, they appeared as a single collective entity—a great serpent of warriors, a single untidy line of men no longer roaming in small groups. Here and there, chieftains and noblemen were distinctly visible riding on horseback in scattered intervals along the line.

Onwards they went, climbing high into the west moors, covering more ground with every pagan step into western Christendom. No shame intruded upon their consciences as they passed deserted villages, nor any guilt for the land's torment. Theirs was a quest for personal gain, glory and recognition among their gods.

In the distance, two Celtic men on stationary horses were observing the army as it twisted and curled its way across the marshy terrain. One was a warrior, thickset with dark features, his black hair hanging from the crown of his head in a single, ropelike plait. His long, pointed moustache gave him a fierce appearance, which was only softened by deep brown eyes that blazed with the wisdom of his forty years.

The other was a small frail-looking Christian priest, whose own blue eyes burned with a fervent hatred for the pagan invaders. Pulling his brown hood over his hairless head, he sat upon his mount and muttered in Latin. The sight beyond transfixed him. His dangling legs and fluttering robes were the only signs of movement. After a time, he ventured to talk.

"Do you think they will make the river before nightfall, Caradoc?"

"Yes, they will, Brother Morton," replied the warrior. "The signs could not be more in our favour if we wanted them to." He harbored intolerance towards the old priest, who always seemed to have to add further words to his answers. It was as though he thought everyone imperfect.

"It is God's work," replied Brother Morton eagerly.

Caradoc ignored the added words. Irritated, he turned his mount and disappeared beyond the rocks to negotiate the steep hills, while the old priest remained watchful for a moment longer before following.

He quickly caught up with the warrior and both descended the last part of the scarp together. "Will all the preparations be done in time?" asked the old priest.

"As ready as we can." It was not an answer and he knew it would not satisfy the intrusive Brother Morton, but he did not care.

Once into the gullies, the way became a little easier and Caradoc was able to talk more. "A long day's march would be tiring for any army. If then, at the end of the day, the Saxons were forced to fight for the river, then we would have them at a disadvantage. Many of our men could be deployed on the Saxon side of the river with the water at their backs to prevent the enemy from gaining a much-needed rest.

"These Saxons have no solid leadership. They are all controlled by petty chieftains, although individually, they are good fighting men, their discipline will be lapse at a large collective level. This we can use to our advantage in battle. The experienced warriors might see the river crossing as a trap, but their shouts will die unnoticed amid an unruly mob.

"We know we are outnumbered, but if we fight to a battle plan and keep the upper hand during the early stages, then, when the tide of battle begins to change in the Saxon's favour, which it will, we withdraw our forces into the waiting dusk. The night will swallow us up, enabling our forces to escape into the dark sanctuary of the moors we know so well."

"It will not be easy," cut in the old priest.

"I know! There is much to prepare and time is limited. We must fight a defensive battle and one we will need to retire from, but we must hold them until nightfall." For a moment, he felt doubt over what the future might hold—but then his natural optimism took over as he kicked his mount and coaxed it on with renewed vigour.

***

The advancing Saxon army slowly progressed further into the moors, towards the very river where, unknown to them, Caradoc's Dumnonian army was waiting to engage them in battle.

Travelling at the rear of the pagan horde were Leofstan and his small band of men, accompanied by the priest from the camp of Fulcher. Aldred and Sighelme rode side by side, matching their horses' walking pace to that of the men on foot.

It was an awkward arrangement, so the young horsemen and footmen were conversing with one another, speculating noisily about the outcome of future battles. There was no social discrimination between them—class structure was determined only by the possessions which each warrior carried about his person.

The two cousins with their mounts and fine weaponry, displayed an outward appearance of wealth, even though Sighelme was careless in his dress, not quite fitting the standards of the average freeman. The warriors on foot varied in their dress and weapons:

most had swords and crudely-made shields, some wore their hair loose while others had leather headgear. Leofstan alone wore a helmet of wood, which was encased in a netlike, metal frame.

Poorest among them was Wilfred. Back on Saxon lands, he had been a mere servant to Sighelme. His Celtic mother had died young and in misery as a slave to her Saxon master. She had been abused unmercifully during her time in captivity, which was how she had her son, Wilfred. Wilfred knew nothing of his parents, except that his mother was a Celt and his father a Saxon, and bore no malice against his overlords for the way his mother had been treated. He had grown and lived among them. Half his blood had right of claim to them and in spirit, he was wholly Saxon. When Wilfred had heard of the invasion, he had pleaded with Sighelme for the right to renounce his Celtic blood and go along with his true people, to show his allegiance by fighting for them. When Leofstan granted his permission, he had promised Wilfred his freedom if he proved himself worthy in battle.

All he carried were a battered old shield lined with leather, a spear and a small scramasax—the single-edged knife given to him by Sighelme before the invasion and which he cherished above all his meagre possessions. Walking proudly with the rest of his folk, he had tried anxiously to be heard during the warriors' frequent discussions; his newfound social position inhibited him not at all. It was only when he fell silent, lost in his own thoughts that he was noticed.

Sighelme gazed down upon the youth feeling an unyielding responsibility towards him. The servant boy had undergone a metamorphosis due to his new independence. Sighelme was pleased he had made such self-sufficiency possible. He felt that it was he— and he alone—who had unleashed the strong, determined fighting spirit now inspiring his servant.

"Would you not share your thoughts with us, Wilfred?"

The lad looked up at his master, friend and guardian with a smile, for the tone of voice had carried not only jestful accusation, but also an invitation to relieve himself of worry.

Accepting the offer, he said, "I was thinking of King Ceawlin's anger at us for invading against his will. He prophesied good omens for a spring invasion only."

"And bad omens for the autumn," added Cuthbert, suddenly interested.

Turnstan added, "The king is tied up with matters on Mercia's borders."

"Matters he is settling by talk," spat his brother Rhinehold, a hot-headed young man of action.

Sighelme chuckled. "I think Wilfred has stoked a few fires."

Finally, Aldred spoke, "Ceawlin is a fair-weather fighter." His blatant contempt for the king was obvious. "These people," he resumed, nodding his head towards the west, "brought much hardship upon us when their ruler was alive, yet did Ceawlin bring his forces to help us? No, he did not, and now that an opportunity arises to strike a blow, our king, in his infinite wisdom, decides to allow our foe time to settle his internal problems by invading in the spring."

All eyes were now on him, and for a while, nobody spoke.

Ahead, Leofstan stopped and turned his mount. He was becoming uneasy about his son's apparent excitement and curious to know what caused it.

"Careful, Aldred," whispered Sighelme. "If your father hears such open contempt for the king, he may become angry, for although his own opinions of the monarch are not complimentary, he will not tolerate open disrespect towards him."

"Yes, you are right. Thank you, Sighelme. I allow my passions to run wild sometimes." Aldred sighed, trying to bury his resentment, then quietly and calmly, he continued, "Time and again we debate these issues as we, 'The defiant Gewisse', trudge on into these moorlands and it always seems to come to a head over our king's rejection of our undertaking. It does cause much ill-tempered resentment against him."

"Agreed," whispered Sighelme. "Your father is coming."

Leofstan rode towards them and turned his mount to fall in beside them. "Aldred, Sighelme," he demanded authoritatively, "come, I wish you to ride with the priest and me."

Aldred was quick to obey and so was Sighelme, but not before giving the others a look of dread.

For a short time, Leofstan lingered, studying the small group of men before him but saying nothing. His community was a small one, in which every man was known to him by name. Regarded by the young as a distant character, if ever he did speak to them, it was invariably to vent his harsh temper, so they normally kept quiet when with him, which suited him well.

With a rough kick, he directed and trotted off up the line to where Aldred and Sighelme had fallen in beside the pagan priest.

"They're in for it, now," whispered Cuthbert.

"I think they might get away with the silent treatment if they keep their mouths shut," added Rhinehold.

Turnstan squinted and peered ahead, focusing on Aldred and Sighelme. After satisfying himself that all was well between them and Leofstan, he allowed his gaze to scan the moors for a while. "They seem to be alright," he reassured them nonchalantly.

No one replied. Instead, the young men left walked on in silence, preferring their own thoughts for now.

CHAPTER FOUR

Some miles ahead of the advancing Saxons, sunlight sparkled on the river where the Dumnonian army was desperately making preparations to meet the oncoming invaders. On the western side of the river, and furthest from the enemy, peasants were digging into the marshy ground, piling the sod carefully in front of a trench. Others dug up neat square clumps of turf, which they placed upon the growing mound. The women were preparing weapons for their men as well as themselves. There was an apprehension etched in every Celtic face, but also a resolve that something had to be done.

By late afternoon, the huge peat mound on the west bank had been completed, its surface decorated with turf and even bushes to make it look like a natural feature. Behind it, hundreds of peasants sat waiting, men and women armed with their newly-made bows and various farming implements.

On the other side of the river, the Saxon side, Caradoc had lined up his warriors to meet the oncoming army. Another large contingent of peasants, also armed with bows, had been dispersed behind the defensive line he had formed.

Brother Morton's frail, old body leaned over his mount's mane. "I am most impressed by the mound." He looked back across the river. "It is most ingenious, Caradoc."

The Gwentman frowned and looked to the eastern approach, from where the Saxons would come.

"This part of the plan must succeed if we are to use that deception to our advantage." He nodded his head towards the Dumonian warriors. "They must entice, then retreat across the river in as orderly a fashion as possible."

"Will our men clash with theirs before the retreat?"

Caradoc looked up. "Yes. It is imperative we do."

The old priest looked concerned. "Our force is considerably small to meet their entire army."

"Yes it is. I am giving them the odds at the beginning and these," he pointed to the Dumonian warriors. "Are the most stout-hearted of our warriors. Behind them are bowmen, as you can see. Do you know the Saxon people rarely use the bow and arrow, and their apparent disregard for the weapon has, on occasion, lost them battles in the past? Their custom is close, hand-to-hand fighting. The first engagement will be on our terms, then before they can recover, we slip back to the opposite bank and wait for the second encounter, which will also be on our terms."

"And then hopefully, the night will come," added Brother Morton. He nodded his head. "It will be splendid if the plan works."

"We have rafts waiting at the water's edge for our planned retreat across the river. I would have liked to have made some trial runs at this, for I am not altogether confident of the peasants' steadiness and orderliness in matters of urgency, but there has been no opportunity."

The old priest turned to look eastwards. "Your lookout is riding back. I fear the hour is upon us, Caradoc, and with it, the Saxon army."

"This is the time," Caradoc muttered. Their eager talking ceased abruptly and he turned to the assembled warriors. "Be silent! I command you to clasp your hands in prayer. The Holy Brother Morton," he continued, pointing to the small, frail priest who had been with him all day, "wishes to ask for God's blessing, that we be granted victory in our hour of need over this un-Christian foe."

The self-styled chieftain dismounted and knelt down as the priest began praying. Only a small group of monks around him understood his prayers, as he recited them in Latin. The warriors and peasantry knew only the word "amen". When Brother Morton was finished, he made the sign of the cross and the monks began singing hymns to the now spiritually eager Dumnonians.

***

To the east, a group of horsemen rode furiously to inform the main Saxon army that the enemy had been sighted and the news caused great excitement as it passed rapidly down the line. The various chieftains broke away from their clans and rode to the head of the column, eager for news—Leofstan was among them.

The untidy line of men came to a ragged halt because of the clan chieftains gathered at their head. Enjoying the spectacle of their mounted lords jostling and butting in their eagerness to be close to their leader, some of the warriors found it difficult to contain their amusement. Ahead, horses began neighing and one reared as the confused melee of leaders pushed and contended to be close to Arfast.

One chieftain stood away from the confused mass, amused at his equals' folly. He was laughing so much, the foot warriors thought he might fall from his saddle as he let out high-pitched jovial shrieks of laughter. It became infecious and ran wildly along the column.

"Who is that chieftain?" asked Wilfred.

Sighelme chuckled. "His name is Dunstan."

"Known as Dunstan the Rogue," added Turnstan.

Not to be outdone, Rhinehold threw in his comment. "A veteran of many campaigns against the Dumnonians, and all of them defeats."

"There was no longer any arrogance in him, or his clansmen," said Cuthbert.

They watched as Dunstan called to his men, while pointing to the confused pack of horses and noblemen. He roared a heavy, throaty laugh. His followers immediately took it up, much to the annoyance of Dunstan's peers, but it had boosted the men's morale.

Presently, riders began to break away from the throng and as red-faced overlords began to return to their respective commands, their groups of men gradually ceased their laughter.

Leofstan fell in beside Aldred and Sighelme, who were each struggling to suppress inner laughter. To that end, they pretended not to notice their lord's return, but continued with an apparently interminable conversation about the plant life of the moors.

Only the priest seemed unaware of what was going on. "Did you manage to get any news about the enemy sighting?" he asked. Unwittingly, he almost started the whole company of men off into laughter again, and only the thought of provoking Leofstan too far held them in check.

The embarrassed chieftain cleared his throat. "They are preparing to meet us in battle today." That roused the men's interest and soon, they were discussing it without any heed of the recognised formalities in the presence of the noblemen. They even questioned Leofstan himself on the matter.

The western sun formed a fine backdrop to the Celtic Christian ranks as they prepared to defend, but to the Saxons, the sight was less than impressive. A small, but well-organised, army of Dumnonians formed a line of defence at the foot of a mound. Beyond the ranks of the warriors, about four hundred archers awaited the command to string their bows. Saxons began to fan out across the top of the moor facing them, and many sat down on the grass while the chieftains began to congregate in small groups to discuss their method of attack.

The invaders guessed Caradoc was hoping to hit and run, using the river as a means of escape. They were unaware that a second force was on the opposite bank ready to aid his retreat, for the Celtic earthwork was not visible from where they stood.

The Saxon warriors were lounging on the grass, seemingly confident about the task that lay before them; after all, the stronghold they had stormed the day before had visually shown a much more impressive defence.

"On first hearing of the enemy army awaiting us, I had been agitated, but what stands before us quenches any future fear of Caradoc," said Aldred.

"We'll smash through their ranks in the first charge," agreed Sighelme.

As Leofstan and his two elder nobles rode up, the younger men got to their feet.

"We're going to attack in three sections," he said. "The middle force will engage the enemy on this side of the river, while the two flanking groups go around and cross to the other bank to cut off their retreat. We shall fight with the middle section."

Leofstan fell silent and regarded his men. Most were very young and he was overwhelmed by a fatherly need to protect them. Quietly, he went on, "The coming challenge will be paid for, perhaps by members of our community. Should Woden see fit to take lives from us in sacrifice for victory, then Valhalla's gates will be open for you, but only if courage and determination go with you in battle."

A brief silence fell upon the group and for an instant, there was a bridge of understanding and warmth between them and their leader. All were suddenly bonded in spirit and the quest for victory.

For Wilfred, the unity that followed the speech came as a gratifying pleasure, which flooded him with a brotherly love for his companions. Together, they had become a single entity of spiritual caring, of which he was now a vital part: a small fragment who served to make the group complete.

Down in the distance, the Dumnonian army waited for the onslaught. The chanting of the Christian priests had faded into silence as they watched the pagan hoard before them.

The Saxon footmen now stood in tiny groups according to their clan, each headed by their mounted chieftain.

Further down the hill, a line of men sat patiently on horseback awaiting the command to attack, among them Aldred and Sighelme, together with two older men of high esteem, Hubert and Lambert.

The Saxon high priest in his fluttering white robes and long, grey hair swept back behind him, stood on a peak above the army, his disciples gathered around him. He took a thick, silver chain bearing a silver pendant of a man with an eight-legged horse and grasped it in both hands. With a slow, delicate ease, he raised it high above his head and, staring at it, bellowed forth a plea to the blustering wind.

"In passion, hate, strength and pain,
may Woden's rage possess us.
With malice, spite and taste for blood,
will Woden's hand guide us.
Our desire to kill, our vengeance to flow,
bring Woden's glory upon us."

As he finished, the warrior congregation began to beat their shields with their weapons, creating a crude musical rhythm and chanted, "Woden's glory to us, Woden's glory to us…" incessantly.

To the watching Christian opponents, it was a dance of blasphemy—perhaps Satan himself was running among the Saxon ranks.

Some horses tried to pull away from their Celtic masters and neighed in terror at the rolling sound of swords banging against shields. The noise was panning out across the gully, but the Dumnonians held their mounts, resolutely whispering words of comfort and gently stroking their beasts to try and console them.

Gradually, the chanting increased in intensity and the Saxon footmen began to shuffle about as if in a possessed trance. Men rushed from their groups to where small flocks of sheep had been tethered, screaming and hacking at the terrified beasts.

Caradoc and the old Christian priest stared at the rampaging Saxons. "It's their way of evoking Woden's rage to possess them," said the warrior.

"Does the spectacle not horrify you?" asked the priest, disturbed by Caradoc's apparent liberal manner.

"Only the fact that the sheep being sacrificed belong to us," he replied, turning his mount away, to bring the matter to a close. "They have now got their tempers pitched," he added as he rode off. "The attack will follow shortly."

He was right. In an explosion of high-pitched screams, the mounted section surged towards the small but determined wall of Celtic warriors, whose long spears protruded from their line at an angle of forty-five degrees, inhospitable to any horse.

Behind the spears, about four hundred archers waited on a slope, where they had a clear view of the advancing army, on whom they were now taking aim. The earth beneath their feet seemed to tremble as the hooves of the advancing horde grew louder and the strain showed in their faces as they fought to steady their nerves.

"Hold steady," called Caradoc to the bowmen, his arm raised.

The Saxons had almost reached the first line of defence when he screamed his order.

"NOW!" he roared as four hundred shafts whistled above the heads of the spearmen—cutting spitefully through the sky to descend into the advancing enemy mass, which thundered to a stop like a rolling wave that can't make it further upon the sands.

Curses and screams raged as horses went down, spilling their human burdens over their heads. Men were hurled from their mounts as tiny thudding sounds told of pierced flesh. The chargers following from the rear tripped and stumbled on those who had already fallen.

Had the Saxons spread themselves out, the volley of arrows would have been less deadly, but their plan had been to use a concentrated mass of men to break the defensive wall.

Amid the confusion, a second volley of arrows descended and a gap opened within the Saxon wall.

"Horsemen to me!" bellowed Caradoc. And with sword raised, he led out a small force of riders, hoping to take advantage of the Saxon disarray.

At a shouted order on the opposite hill, the multitude of Saxon footmen surged forward, but Caradoc's ambitious charge reached its goal before any of the enemy footmen had covered a quarter of the distance.

In the midst of the carnage, Aldred painfully picked himself up. He remembered looking over his horse's head as the grass came up to meet him after the first volley of arrows, but nothing more. Now Celtic horsemen were hacking away at his dazed countrymen. The unexpected presence of the Dumnonians among his own ranks unnerved him. The possibility of defeat had been so far removed from his mind, that the facts before him seemed sinister and uncanny. It was as though his eyes were deceiving him and he watched in abstract horror as his countrymen were chopped and hacked before him. Amid the screams and confusion, he was no longer the arrogant young warrior who had traveled the wilderness alone to be with his father and kin, for now, a wretched animal seemed to be fighting within him to take over his senses. Boldly, he fought the inner battle while he stood by his dead horse—the fighting and killing raging around him.

CHAPTER FIVE

A Celtic horseman rode past and struck down a Saxon who, like Aldred, was recovering from a fall. With gritted teeth and determined thoughts of a kill to put himself back in touch with the battle, Aldred ran at the enemy with sword raised and delivered a mighty blow. A blood-curdling scream emitted as the Celt momentarily stiffened, then fell apart within the blood-soaked garments that feebly contained the chopped body. Dead meat splattered to the earth, and Aldred took one more savage swing and his spatha smashed into the dead skull in an almighty explosion of blood and gore. He grunted with effort and his blood-splattered face wore a look of disgust as he pulled the blade free amid the splintered bone fragments.

The sound of a horn filled the air and at once, the Dumnonians withdrew to their defensive position.

Aldred looked down at the dead and wounded around him. The Dumnonians had devastated the Saxon charge with hardly any loss of life to themselves—the only dead Celt he could see was the man lying at his feet. At that moment, Aldred lost the naivety of youth. He had never imagined such things happening to the Saxons and he found he viewed the sufferings of his own countrymen in quite a different light from those of the Dumnonians the day before. These dead men were from nearby villages; he had known some of them as boys.

A small number of Saxons were still on their own mounts, while others were clambering onto those of dead warriors. Sighelme and Hubert were there, with Lambert, whose chin was sunk onto his chest, both hands clasping at his bloodstained clothing. Hubert, beside him, was trying to prop him upright.

Shakily, Sighelme asked Aldred, "Are you all right?"

Nodding, Aldred asked with concern, "What happened to Lambert?"

"He was hit in the chest by an arrow," explained Hubert, "we'd better lay him down here." The stricken man was gently lifted from his horse and, as they wrapped his cloak around him, Lambert's tired, glazed eyes opened. A smile creased his face as he recognised the worried features of his old friend. They had shared a lifetime together and both were now past forty. The smile faded as his eyes closed for the last time.

Hubert stood up with an expression of grief. Gruffly, he said to Aldred, "You'd better take Lambert's horse." All three then mounted and resumed the attack alongside their footmen, who had now caught up.

Only the central contingent of Saxon footmen had engaged directly with the solid body of Celts, the rest running past the conflicting mass on either side with the aim of crossing the river. This was to cut off any chance of an enemy retreat, for they still had thoughts of a total massacre of the small force of Celtic warriors and peasants.

***

Caradoc was now organizing his retreat. One section of his force was still locked in a pitched battle with the Saxons, while the bowmen crossed on crudely-made rafts firing arrows into the enemy, who were trying to swim over to cut them off.

Concealed on the opposite bank, the force of peasant bowmen were hard put to keep their patience as they waited for the enemy, but on the other side of the river, the Saxons' fortunes were beginning to change. In the fierce hand-to-hand combat, many Celts were falling and slowly, the defending mass began to retreat. Some stout-hearted peasants lingered behind the defensive wall to shoot arrows into the Saxon mass wherever they seemed to be gaining too much of an upper hand. This won the defenders more time to reorganise themselves.

***

Aldred, Sighelme and Hubert, in the thick of it, found being mounted was now a hindrance in the battle raging so closely around them. Accordingly, Aldred and Sighelme discarded their horses, but Hubert, whose horse represented a significant proportion of his wealth, remained mounted. He was among the few who managed to break through the Celtic line. Finding himself vulnerable in open ground, he looked around, anxious to claim a kill when suddenly, an old Christian priest stumbled in front of him.

***

Brother Morton had been un-horsed and was desperately trying to scramble down to the river. He looked up in horror as the old Saxon horseman loomed before him with sword drawn and a scream of triumph. The pagan's battle cry served to alert Brother Morton to the danger and he turned to meet his attacker.

Wrinkled fingers tightened around the long-staffed crucifix and the old priest's eyes blazed with a fierce longing to kill the approaching invader, a violater of all he loved and believed in. He waited until the horse was almost upon him, then jumped to one side, escaping the Saxon's sword. As the Saxon rode harmlessly by, the priest swung his cross sharply up and into the horseman's unprotected back.

***

Hubert felt a violent pain that caused his entire body to jerk spasmodically. He dropped his sword and shield and put both hands behind his back, feeling a gaping wound. As he slid to the ground, knocking himself unconscious, a group of Dumnonian peasants came to Brother Morton's aid and pounced upon Hubert and hacked the life from him in a brutal frenzy.

***

Caradoc's men retreated to the river's edge, some fighting waist deep in water in an effort to prevent total encirclement. Some Dumnonians, who had safely reached the opposite side of the river, were now forming defensive groups with the aim of repelling the enemy flanks on either side of the central struggle. It was imperative that the Saxons not gain a foothold.

Rapidly assessing the situation, Caradoc could see it was time for the next stage.

"To the river!" he cried at the top of his voice.

At his shouted command, his men suddenly turned and plunged into the river.

***

The Saxon warriors were quite confounded by the swiftness of Caradoc's withdrawal. One moment, they were fighting against resolute and desperate men; the next instant, they were gone in a flurry of spray, their swords and shields abandoned on the ground.

Overcoming their astonishment, the Saxons were soon pursuing them and heading for their next goal: to breach the western riverbank, dealing savagely with the enemy's mortally wounded as they trampled and hacked over them where they were huddled together on the shingle.

Gaining the temporary safety of the western bank, Caradoc screamed aloud.

"All up and fight, now!"

The reserve force came from behind the mound, screaming like demons escaping from an underworld confine, and swarmed down upon the drenched enemy. By the time Caradoc had managed to organise them, the Saxons were already emerging from the river.

Rearmed and ready to do battle, the Dummonian warriors were confident in the knowledge they had already inflicted a severe blow. Aware that some among them were ready to rush straight in for the kill, Caradoc cried, "Let them come onto the shore first." Gearing himself up for the next onslaught of violence, he continued muttering to himself, "Let them come to us."

The first invaders waded ashore, exhausted after swimming the river with their weapons, and advanced wearily upon Caradoc's force.

Tired blows were easily blocked as the defenders' counterblows bit into unprotected ankles. Shrill screams rent the air as Saxons went down in agony.

"Forward!" shouted Caradoc, and Dumnonian warriors leapt over their injured foes, allowing the following peasants to fall upon the stricken Saxons and hack the wounded men to death. Crude farming tools rudely came down upon the wretched bodies, cutting and smashing the souls from them. Saxons still in the water could only look on in horror and attempt a more cunning approach to Caradoc's advanced preparations.

***

Aldred was among a group who had scrambled ashore further upstream. The men ahead of him were either dead or fighting desperately at the riverbank's edge in order to hold some ground.

He rose from the water to meet a young Celt, poised and ready for combat, his expression clearly showing his determination to kill the enemy.

Shaking his wet locks away from his head, Aldred stared at his opponent, noting his inexperience in waiting for him to stand instead of striking him as he crawled up the bank.

With sword raised, the Celt came forward, but Aldred thwarted the blow with his shield held above his head whilst slashing fiercely at his opponent's side, only to feel the thud of metal striking wood.

They unlocked from the brief contact and circled warily, each watching for a weakness—an opening. Aldred no longer had any consciousness of the battle around him; all his senses were engaged in his own combat.

A low swipe was aimed at Aldred's ankle, but he was able to block it, for once again, his opponent forewarned him by looking at the point of attack before striking.

Aldred was quite unprepared for the next move. His assailant followed his blocked strike with a hard barge of his shield. The boss smashed into his midriff, winding him and knocking him off balance and back into the murky river.

As the waters closed over him, mud and stones churned up as his hands and feet kicked out in a frantic effort to keep himself below the surface, so he would not give his position away. His eyes stopped stinging, but he was gripped by panic and fear. He'd have to go up soon for air.

Suddenly, there was another eruption of mud, stones and bubbles beside him, and as it began to settle, he saw the fur boots and breeches of his opponent.

The desperate Saxon's hand fumbled for the scramasax at his hip. Nervously, excitedly, his fingers tightened around the long knife's hilt.

Smashing through the surface as though he was a soul escaping from the underworld, Aldred took the life of the Dumnonian with ruthless efficiency.

Panting for breath, he was overcome by dizziness. A firm but reassuring hand gripped his arm and he heard Turnstan ask, "Are you injured, Aldred?"

"No," he gasped awkwardly, "I'm unharmed."

Cuthbert and Rhinehold were with Turnstan and now they all waded towards the enemy bank where the fierce struggle was continuing. Shouts and screams rose from the murderous multitude, with metal crashing against metal, chopping into wood and severing flesh.

Beyond the line of combat on the Dumnonian side stood Sighelme. He had battled through the enemy defenses and into the mass of oncoming peasants, only to find himself in great peril. The young Saxon swung his sword and blocked with his shield to great effect. Two peasants lay slain at his feet and now his remaining assailants were being a bit more wary before striking out at him, encircling him and conversing in their strange tongue.

The gray arc of the flashing spatha came to another bloody halt amid an explosion of red gore, sending a third body crashing to the marshy, green turf. Sighelme broke out of the mob, only to see an enemy warrior running at him. He ducked as the barbed spear went harmlessly over his head and the Dumnonian, unable to stop, crashed into him. Sighelme felt a sharp pain in his ribs as he was bowled over and a moment later, he was lying on his back. The face of a peasant momentarily loomed over him, silhouetted against the dull blue evening sky, before being thrust aside by another dark-limbed figure. Scrambling to his feet, Sighelme saw Wilfred standing over the corpse of another peasant, gasping for breath after the fatiguing ordeal of killing the Celt.

"I owe you my life," said Sighelme, looking into the youth's determined face.

Wilfred glanced around him, saw they were safe and smiled. "Your willing servant and companion," he replied.

Sighelme put his hand upon Wilfred's shoulder and gripped him warmly. Together, they went back into battle, side by side.

***

The brown steed barged through the retreating wall of Dumnonians, carrying Leofstan into the melee behind.

He had not gone far when his horse suddenly reared and let out a choked snort. The beast toppled sideways, flinging its rider to the ground, and as it lay upon his side in a final death throe, Leofstan tried to stand. He was on his knees when a peasant came screaming towards him. Instinctively, Leofstan raised his sword, but the thin young Celt sent it spinning from his hand. Again the peasant swung at Leofstan, only to impale his crude weapon upon the wood of Leofstan's shield.

With a sudden desperate surge, Leofstan sprang to his feet and threw his fist forward over his shield, punching his enemy in the face. The force of the blow lifted the young assailant off his feet, throwing him onto his back.

As Leofstan looked for his sword, a sharp pain racking into his leg convulsed him. Above his knee protruded an arrow, blotched by a red ring of blood that stained his faded and worn tanned breeches. He staggered back a step and fell down upon the knee of the wounded leg, his face contorted with pain. As he struggled to remove the barbed head, his life was swiftly taken with a precise thrust from a spear-brandishing warrior. The chieftain's back arched inwards and he let out a furious roar of pain as he jerked up to the heavens in open-mouthed surprise. He was momentarily convulsed in a spasm as his assailant—wickedly grinning through gritted teeth, twisted the spearhead inside his body, tearing, ripping and entwining his innards.

Leofstan's last high-pitched agonizing scream tore out into the air before he mercifully fell forward onto the turf, where he died grateful, perhaps, his kin had not seen his wretched demise.

***

One of the peasants picked up the dead chieftain's sword and fell in alongside the rest of his order, who were now making for the sanctuary of the moors.

The setting sun hovered upon the horizon dragging the daylight with it, allowing the blackness of night to settle upon the two armies, hampering the task of one and aiding the retreat of the other.

Caradoc's remaining men ran off into the waiting dusk, leaving the demoralised Saxons unwilling to pursue as their zeal for battle had deserted them.

CHAPTER SIX

Burning torches flickered in the cold blackness of the night as the Saxons searched deep in the gloom for their wounded countrymen. Those warriors who had emerged from the conflict unscathed were determined to help their fallen comrades as best they could. The wounded were treated, the mortally injured were brought back to die in comparative comfort by the big campfires or, if they suffered too much to be moved, they were swiftly put out of their agony. There were even those who had managed to survive gruesome amputations. Among the search parties were the survivors from Leofstan's band who had received word of his demise.

Cuthbert hung his head in sorrow for his father and the others of the clan. "Time and again we have heard the tales of battle around the campfires; stories of bravery and honor, lavishly dressed in mystical romance by the gripping voices of our bards. The heroic egotism of those stories seems far removed from the reality of battle we are now experiencing." He looked up at Aldred with tears in his eyes. "We've lost all our elders."

"Apart from the elders, Edgar was slain at the riverbank," announced Aldred, grief-stricken. "This entire battle has been a crushing blow to us all."

The others nodded their demoralized heads in agreement. They looked about them and listened to moans that came from the other clans who were scattered about by their various campfires.

"Thank the Gods our kinsman were swiftly released," said Rhinehold. "I would hate to have seen our people in such suffering."

Turnstan looked to Aldred and asked, "How will we continue now we are deprived of our senior men?"

Sighelme stood up, struggling inwardly with his grief. At last, he managed to compose himself. "I think we had better go out and look for Leofstan's body," he said, glancing down at the corpses of Hubert and Edgar. "Lambert, we know is on the other side of the river where we left him. I would feel more settled if we could find our Lord's body."

"Yes, so would I," agreed Aldred sadly. "Let us be about this unpleasant task."

Lighting torches from the campfire, they set off to search accompanied by some of Dunstan's men who had brought the news of Leofstan's death.

Eventually, they came upon their chieftain's body, lying on his stomach with his head turned to the left. His eyes and mouth were open as though studying and eating the grass at the same time. His horse lay by him, with blood congealed from a gaping wound in its neck. Aldred knelt down and turned his father's body over onto his back. Resting his hand upon the dead man's face, the skin felt cold. Finally, he closed the dead man's eyes and stood up, allowing Wilfred, Rhinehold and Turnstan to carry the body back to camp.

***

Throughout the night, specks of light flared up around the Saxon camp. High in the western hills, Celtic watchmen looked down upon the lights, among them, Caradoc and Brother Morton, who sat on a rock eating cold mutton under the half moon, while their followers went about their duties.

"You have done well for these people, Caradoc. God shines good fortune upon them through you," remarked the old priest as he was about to take another bite from his meal. His tone was more pleasant than usual.

"Your holiness is more than kind in his praise," replied Caradoc, not wishing to argue with him. For a moment, there was a bridge of understanding between them.

"It is the simple truth, Caradoc."

The warrior looked into the priest's icy blue eyes and then allowed a smile to crease his face as his gaze wandered back down into the hollow where the enemy were camped. After a while, he ventured to speak again. "There may yet be more fighting, holy father, if our Saxon foes decide to advance further. We dealt them a hard blow this evening, much harder than I'd expected, but their heads are thick and they are taking rather a long time to realize they are beaten."

"Are they beaten?" asked the priest.

"Not yet," answered Caradoc. "But they will be before long if they keep on trying to advance. As we harass them, wear them down, their numbers will gradually decrease, while ours will grow daily as more of our people rally to the cause."

"Yes," said the priest excitedly, "perhaps we shall be able to chase them all the way back to their ancestral grounds in the Rhinelands."

"We may at that, holy father, we may at that," laughed Caradoc.

Down in the valley, work continued under cover of darkness. Aldred, now chieftain, sat silently with his followers by a small fire. All except Turnstan stared into the flames crackling among the dead bracken and leaves. They lost themselves in the blaze, finding some sad form of tranquility. Turnstan tried to sleep, but the thought of the continued quest plagued him miserably. He looked to Aldred and Cuthbert and felt sympathy for them. Both had lost a father and, like the rest of them, they had to fight on.

"We will need to dig deep and find a great deal of courage," he muttered.

Cuthbert looked to him. "But our efforts have not brought us victory."

"Fortune declares we should continue with this," said Aldred, grim faced and biting back tears.

"Aldred, may I talk with you?" asked a husky, sorrowful voice from beyond the campfire and the young chieftain looked up into the face of Dunstan the Rogue.

The old man's happy-go-lucky manner had deserted him. There was sympathy in his eyes as he stared down at the little group. Long, matted gray hair hung down well past his shoulders. He wore a long-sleeved dark patterned frock over gray breeches with striped leggings up to his knees. From his shoulders and wrapped across his chest was a light gray cloak with green and gold patterning that ran along the short tasseled edge.

Immediately getting to his feet, Aldred politely replied, "Yes, of course," and began to seek somewhere more private.

"What I have to say need not be excluded from the men, Aldred," said Duncan, "but, of course, if you wish to hear me in private, I..."

"No, it's all right, we'll speak here, thank you, Dunstan," interrupted Aldred.

Unaccustomed to conventional manners, the old war dog nonetheless, felt he should make an effort and smiled gratefully when Aldred invited him to sit. There were a few polite offerings of food and drink, all of which Dunstan refused. When he had the group's attention, he began to talk.

"In the morning, we shall bury our dead. The priests will conduct a short ceremony, after which they will ask us to continue with the invasion. They will make the usual speeches about the victory we have won in battle."

Aldred looked at the old chieftain in some surprise. "Victory?" he mocked.

"Yes, my friend," replied Dunstan. "As far as the priesthood is concerned, we have won a victory. They will find many ways to convince us of that. For a start, they will remind us that the enemy forces were forced to retreat into the darkness..."

"But that was a tactical withdrawal," protested Aldred.

"We all know that," agreed Dunstan, "and so do the priests. But that won't stop them from interpreting it as a victory. Would any of us dare to stand against the word of the High Priest? There will also be the honor of our dead to be taken into account." Aldred frowned and shook his head and Dunstan went on.

"We cannot pretend we expected the losses we have suffered. They are far greater than we thought they would be, especially at such an early stage. We have lost about four hundred men and there are a great many who are too seriously wounded to go any further. We started out with three thousand men, but now, we are down to a fighting force of two thousand three hundred.

"Almost a third of this army has been lost in battle. To the north, Fulcher's army is demoralized and there is talk of withdrawal. It that happens, Egbert and the men who are advancing in the south will retreat as well. Out of a complete invasion force of eighteen thousand men, only our small army will continue."

Aldred was quite shocked by this and so were his men, who began to mutter darkly about the grim prospect of invading alone under the leadership of Arfast.

"How do you come by all this knowledge?" asked Aldred.

"I see and hear what goes on. Some things I'm seeing now are not new—I've seen them before.

"The priests travelling with the other two armies are beginning to leave them in order to join us. You mark my words, tomorrow will bring more of them here."

Somewhat bemused, Aldred asked, "So, what does this mean?"

Dunstan stood and began pacing backwards and forwards. "The invasion is losing its vigor, much to the annoyance of the priesthood—but then, they anticipated it from the start. That is why they organized the invasion by making false claims and telling us how we should go about it.

"The big clans were put together under the direct rule of Fulcher to the north and Egbert in the south, so even if only a few chieftains broke their allegiance to their overlord, chaos would ensue, which in fact, happened when Fulcher was killed. Being disowned by Ceawlin has not helped either, for there's a rumour he may have given leave to his loyal followers to take over our unprotected settlements.

"When Egbert's men heard that, they immediately feared Fulcher's men might attempt the same thing on their return, so there, too, the large clans are beginning to disperse and go home. This army, of course," continued Dunstan, sardonically, "is made up of small clans, so if the odd chieftain decides to pull out, he will only take a small number with him. The priesthood also has a stronger influence over us smaller clans."

"You and your clan never appear to pay much attention to the priests," commented Aldred.

"Yes, that is true," agreed Dunstan. "I have seen too many of my clansmen die because of their doctrine. My father listened to them and lost much of his wealth. There was a time when our clan numbered many, but reckless pursuit of conquest caused us to dwindle.

"My father was killed and I took over the leadership in much the same circumstances as you. Slowly, and with great effort, I managed to rebuild my clan and now I have a warrior force of forty-two men, all but five of them youngsters like yourselves. I was able to build that number by ignoring the priests and their useless talk of sacrifices to Woden."

"If you feel this way, why did you join the invasion?" asked Aldred.

It was a direct, awkward question and Dunstan did not shy away. "There was a chance of plunder, more riches to be gained. When things were going well, it was worth my while to be here. But now, things are not so good. The large clans are leaving. That is how they remain large. In the morning, I, too, will leave, to give my clan a chance to grow a little more. Once, when I was in the same position as you are now, a chieftain from another clan told me the same story as I am telling you. I took heed of his words. When I leave for home, I would like you to come with me."

"I thank you for your advice, Dunstan," said Aldred sincerely, "but you have given me much to think over and discuss with my men."

For a while, there was silence, which was finally broken by Sighelme. Catching Dunstan's attention, he asked, "Gracious Lord, why, if what you say is true, does the priesthood wish us to continue into this land?"

Dunstan snorted. "This army's high chieftain, Arfast, is eating out of the hands of the priesthood. They want him to continue because a Christian monastery lies in our path. Christian missions are sent into our lands from this place and they are beginning to have much influence in parts of our land and Mercia.

"Our priests are very worried about this—they see these Christians threatening the survival of our religion.

"Indeed, these one God people have made a big impression throughout the world. Even once-mighty Rome has succumbed to their beliefs. That is why they want the monastery destroyed."

"Even if we are slaughtered in the attempt?" asked Aldred.

"Yes," replied Dunstan, "and you will be."

"Caradoc is no one's fool. It won't take him long to see this army's intentions. Then he'll hit back.

"More and more Dumnonians will come to his aid now and his force will become bigger than yours. They will gradually wear you down, as is the way of peasant bands. Their warriors will meet you in open conflict and eventually, you'll all be defeated. A few stragglers will make their way home and find their settlements swallowed up by the bigger clans who went back early. Think of the damage to your community if none of you were to return and the male population consisted only of infants."

Aldred pondered on the situation, looking into the fire, lost in thought. "I know what you say is right, Dunstan. Yet I cannot make a decision now."

The old chieftain rose to his feet to return to his own men. "If you're leaving with me, young Aldred, you have until morning to make up your mind."

When he had gone, Aldred looked at his men. "Our choice must be the decision of us all. There are only six of us now, so if we do go back home, I don't think we'd be able to defend our community adequately."

Cuthbert was quick to point out they could not have done much with ten warriors.

"There is a pact among the small bands to pull together and help one another if a larger clan should try to absorb us," said Rhinehold. "If we stay with the rest of our brothers at arms, it will most certainly strengthen our pact with them, and then if it did happen when we returned home, we could tackle it adequately."

Sighelme disagreed, "But it wouldn't be that way. The larger clans would not move until they knew whether or not we were coming back."

The debate went on deep into the night until it was agreed that if a large number of bands decided to follow the example of Dunstan, then Aldred and his men would do the same. They would follow the majority and thus keep within the tribal pact.

A downpour of rain in the morning further hindered the men in their efforts to collect the remainder of the corpses littering the field, but after much struggling, all the dead were laid to rest in a long grave.

A large number of priests came into the camp from the other two armies, just as Dunstan had predicted, and when the burial ceremony began, there was a congregation of more than seventy priests. The old High Priest stood in front of them at the side of the mass grave. Opposite, the wet and bedraggled army waited in silence.

The High Priest looked up into the dull, overcast sky, his hands outstretched in supplication to the gods to look down upon the humble congregation before them.

"Oh, Woden, take unto thy domain these worthy men,
Give them a place in Valhalla for your needs,
For they have delivered themselves unto you,
Your glory for theirs, in exchange."

After the short prayer, he began to shake seeds and herbs from a small casket into the grave. Then followed more prayers, to other gods—Thunder, Ty and Frigg, to which the warriors listened respectfully.

Having finished his blessing, the old priest began to hobble along the graveside. Reaching the end, he turned and slowly proceeded back the way he had come. Not until he was halfway back did he begin to call out to the warriors, speaking of their dead countrymen's courageous sacrifice. And on he went, cleverly mixing the invasion effort with religious aims, carefully manipulating the passions of the men before him, pushing them to new heights of determination.

Warriors began to shout out, demanding the continuation of the advance. More began to join in and, before long, the priest had to stop talking. He stood looking at the army before him with a broad, satisfied smile on his face and allowed the clamor to continue.

When the warriors had exhausted themselves, they settled into an uneasy silence as the priest began to talk persuasively of the Christian monastery that lay before them.

Aldred and his men, standing within the massed ranks, looked around at each other. Dunstan had been right in all he had predicted.

CHAPTER SEVEN

Aldred was feeling demoralized, like the rest of his clan, and he stood watching as Sighelme came back from his wandering—he had been trying to find out whether the clans would continue the invasion or retire home. Stopping before Aldred, he sighed and shook his head.

"The priesthood has been successful in persuading most of the clans to stay and continue with the invasion, but it is now too late in the day to advance; they want to remain here until morning. Six groups, including Dunstan's, numbering one hundred and four warriors, have decided to return home."

"I'll have to see Dunstan," replied Aldred despondently. "We must go on—though I admit, I am reluctant."

He left Sighelme with the clan and went to look for Dunstan. He found the old chieftain as he was about to mount his horse. Somber, though not unsympathetic, he looked at the young chieftain. "So, you have decided against leaving with us, Aldred."

"We have, Dunstan, though it is not because we are disrespectful of your counsel. There are other reasons why we wish to continue."

"Yes, I understand these things."

"Before you go," continued Aldred, "I wish to ask of you a great favor. If my men and I should not return, would you take over my community for me?"

He looked surprised. "I would do this for you, Aldred, certainly," said the old chieftain hesitantly, "but how would I make your women and children believe it was your wish? They would surely think I was taking advantage for my own gain."

"Take this ring," said Aldred. "One day, when we were quite alone, my mother and I walked together by the brook outside our village. We talked of many things, including my inheritance of the chieftainship. I promised her that I would always do what I thought was right. After we finished our talk, she gave me this ring. When you see her, tell her that I have done what I believed to be right and then give her the ring. She will then know that you are acting on my wishes."

Dunstan took the ring and studied it. The object was of bronze, with a dragon's head on its face.

"I will go straight to your mother with this," he assured Aldred. "If you come home, I shall hand the village back into your care, but if not, I shall look after the women and children as my own and allow your young boys to become warriors under me when they grow up."

"Thank you, Dunstan." He turned and left the brave old warrior.

***

The news of Caradoc's victory against the Saxons spread across Dumnonia, along with rumours of two main enemy forces withdrawing, encouraging the Celts to unite in their efforts to repel the invaders.

Dumnonian chieftains sent out warriors to swell Caradoc's ranks, and soon, the man from Cymru found himself the overall leader of a great number of chieftains.

The army of Dumnonians was constructed in a very similar way to that of the Saxons, save that Caradoc had the advantage of a great number of peasants at his disposal.

He knew there were disadvantages to this stronger force. He would find difficulty in controlling the newly-arrived chieftains, who would likely criticize his military planning and so his leadership would be less secure than before.

Brother Morton, unknowingly, gave him an idea for dealing with the problem.

Hearing from his scouts of the retreat of the two Saxon armies, Caradoc was confused. "Why should the remaining party wish to continue with the invasion?" he asked.

"We have learned of the influx of pagan priests from the two withdrawing armies, and this one remaining force is obviously influenced by them."

Caradoc's eyes and mouth opened wide as the notion came to him, "They will come upon your monastery."

Brother Morton stood back astounded. "My word, you are correct." He realized what was afoot. "Let us tell the others of this. We must act."

"Be subtle, Brother Morton. I feel it would be wise to suggest the dangers and let them think it is their idea."

The old priest nodded. "You are right, Caradoc. I lack your diplomacy. Would you do the talking?"

"Of course," he smiled. It was his intended idea to do so, but he had suggested the danger of Brother Morton's overexcited approach.

In a small sunlit clearing just outside the Dumnonians' main encampment, Caradoc and Brother Morton met the new group of chieftains and all gathered in debate. It was a very casual affair, with the majority of the group sitting cross-legged upon the carpet of dead leaves, while the others leant against trees.

They felt an urgent need to explain the latest events to the new arrivals. They excitedly planned for the monastery's urgent need of defense and thus Caradoc and Brother Morton were able to manipulate them into their way of thinking. For some time, they debated the issues in the green confine and when the final talking was concluded, Caradoc was not found wanting.

"Some of you have your own ideas on how to meet the situation, and I know all of you are eager to engage the Saxons in open conflict." He paused, knowing that despite their increased numbers, an all-out battle would not be profitable at this stage. "A victory is unlikely at present, and if our men are defeated, the survivors would neither have the capability nor the morale to continue with the struggle. The monastery, obviously the Saxon's goal, would then be doomed to destruction. This is now their only goal. It is all they can achieve, as this small Saxon force could not begin to conclude a successful invasion now—not with just two thousand men.

'I need to pull this force back, further west, down from the moors and into the green forestland. Although autumn is approaching, the trees yet retain their summer splendor. Some of the outlaws of the forest must be promised a pardon, for they would help the cause. Such men can keep watch on the pathways and also lead our fighters to a place of safety and comfortable seclusion."

Shafts of sunlight poured through the branches, brightening up the small areas of woodland in scattered sectors of tranquility. Birdsong brought the forest alive in a grand abundance of life, heard though not seen. The men were surrounded by the hidden, mystical secrets of nature and it was as though the surroundings helped to convey Caradoc's words of advice.

"This morning, the Saxons will be in the forest," he continued. "It would be in our very best interests to prepare for an ambush on the main trackway."

A tall and very broad chieftain named Rhese had something to say. "When first we came to you, Caradoc, you said you wanted a cautious approach to our enemy. In that, I agree with you and generally stand by your good judgement on the matter, but in this instance, I'd like to say the Saxons would be fully alert and watchful for such a surprise ambush, especially within the forest."

Caradoc nodded his head. "That is true, Rhese, your words carry much weight. But in a forest of such magnitude," then clenching his fists to lend strength to his words, he repeated, "a forest of this size still offers ample opportunity to get close enough to the enemy for such attacks. It does not matter if they are on edge and waiting. It would be good for us. Let them worry, let them fear."

"Have we any strategy agreed for that?" asked another warrior.

"Yes," replied Caradoc, "we shall use our peasants for the attack, shooting from among the foliage and concentrating on the enemy's rear. Their whole column will be halted and those at its head will go out into the trees and try to surround our men. To meet this move, we shall make use of our reinforcements. You chieftains will attack these groups trying to encircle us. Of course, we shall have to prepare ourselves to meet the main force for a short time, too. Retaliation is bound to be swift and violent when they see the dilemma their men are in."

"Well," said Rhese, "this is all very similar to your last method of attack. Surely the enemy won't fall for the same trick again?"

Caradoc replied, "The Saxons can either stay put on the pathway and let the peasants fill them with arrows, or else come out to us. Quite honestly, I don't care which approach they adopt. Either way, we stand to profit."

These words seemed to conclude the debate as far as Rhese was concerned. Caradoc's case was unarguable and Rhese could find nothing more to ask; he lapsed into silence. There being no more questions, Caradoc went on to talk about their next plan of attack in more detail.

***

As the Saxon army marched deeper into the Celtlands, they became increasingly gloomy as to what they would gain from their adventure. This was no longer an invasion; now it was merely a small enterprise to destroy a single Christian monastery. The whole offensive had burnt out. All that remained was this small, battle-weary army, made up of low-status clans.

Coming down from the moors towards the forest, the men began nervously conversing among themselves about the awesome possibility of ambush. Caradoc's plan of campaign was becoming all too obvious to them: they were now marching into his domain to fight according to his wishes.

Unlike the Dumnonians, the Saxons viewed the forest as being full of foreboding. Twisted branches loomed over them menacingly, like fingers belonging to the hand of a giant, demented demon; hands, which would come down to clasp them at any sudden moment. At the outset, the Saxons had felt themselves almost indestructible, the Dumnonians' resistance seeming so futile. Now, however, it was they who were dictating the course of war; the inferior Saxons had to comply with their wishes in order to continue with the advance and salvage some gain from their invasion.

"There are far fewer of us mounted now, owing to the loss of horses in the previous battle." Turnstan was looking back along the column.

"You must also count the numbers that have been given to Dunstan in order to make easier his task of carrying back the seriously wounded," added Rhinehold.

Aldred and his five remaining men were all on foot. Recent experiences had brought them even closer and each of them was consoled by the fact five brothers-in-arms cared for his personal safety, just as he, in turn, was devoted to theirs. The small band was no exception to the rest of the army when it came to cleanliness: all of them were absolutely filthy. Long, matted, greasy hair hung over tired, unwashed faces, and black bags sagged under their eyes. Only their begrudged loyalty to the Quest and strong faith in each other enabled their fatigued bodies to find the strength to continue.

Rhinehold rubbed his eyes repeatedly in an effort to remove the grime, but found it to no avail. Turnstan found some amusement in watching him:

"No matter how hard you try, you won't be rid of the sleep without the use of a good wet rag!" he laughed.

"He wouldn't know what one looked like," jeered Sighelme, joining in.

"Really," replied Rhinehold indignantly. Unslinging his leather water bag, he proceeded to dampen a patch of his frock in order to wash his face. Once he had satisfied himself the cloth was wet enough, the haughty young Saxon applied himself to the task with some vigor.

"That's right, take the dirt off your face and put it onto your clothes," began Turnstan in a fresh assault.

Rhinehold maintained his dignity and dryly made it clear that he at least took pains to preserve some measure of cleanliness. The other members of the band began to cheer up and block out the uncomfortable reservations they were beginning to feel in their minds about the forest. Turnstan and Rhinehold were now mocking each other, a frequent occurrence which never failed to amuse its observers. Turnstan always got them on his side when he threw out remarks about Rhinehold's odd little habits. The naïve Rhinehold would take it all so seriously, he would start looking for ways to verbally hit back.

His childlike attempts provoked all manner of laughter from the onlookers, especially when he began to make comments about Turnstan's lack of cleanliness.

Around them, the men jeered and encouraged the brothers on, enjoying the tit for tat banter.

The only person among Aldred's clan not to delight in the rude form of entertainment was Cuthbert. Oblivious to what was going on around him, this young warrior trudged on, lost within the innermost recesses of his mind. His father's death had grieved him deeply and ever since then, he often cut himself off in this way.

Aldred frequently broke off from watching the comical little frolics to observe Cuthbert. Although he sympathized with the distraught young man, having undergone the same experience himself, deep down, Aldred also harbored contempt for Cuthbert. Cuthbert's obvious torment disturbed Aldred, who found he could not grieve in the same way for his own father's death. Perhaps his men would think him an unloving son, to see him apparently so un-lamenting, but he could not help the way he felt. If he could bring back the life of his father, he would, but only a God could perform such feats. The sight of Cuthbert unnerved him, however, racking his wall of logic.

Feeling he ought to say something, he fell in with the young man, a little apart from the others.

"It is difficult, I know, Cuthbert," he began somewhat diffidently, "the death of someone close always brings much heartache." The few brief words were all he felt able to offer and now he wished he had remained silent. The consoling effort had been too half-hearted.

Unbeknown to Aldred, however, his words had allowed Cuthbert an opportunity to speak. "I wish their deaths had been for a more substantial cause, that's all. At first, it was to broaden our kingdom— for glory; but when the king refused to give us his blessing, our original quest was doomed from the start."

"But, Cuthbert," said Aldred, surprised, "the only reason the original aim was unsuccessful was, as you say, the king's lack of support. Many of the inner communities would have rallied to the cause if he had been behind us."

"But he wasn't, was he?" argued Cuthbert. "That is what I am trying to make clear. Our countrymen will not say, 'If the king had supported the invasion, it would surely have succeeded'; they will say, 'The king wisely predicted the outcome from the start'. He will be regarded as a king of great wisdom, while we will become known as the idiots who disobeyed their king's good counselling, to go and die on a fools' quest. Our fathers' names will be among those dead; perhaps ours, too."

"We do have a motive, Cuthbert," said Aldred, trying to give him some encouragement. "The priests have at least given us that hope."

"Aldred," replied Cuthbert in tired sympathy for his chieftain, "do you honestly think our fathers would have risked our lives, just to destroy a Christian monastery? We're all from small communities, too small to risk warriors' lives unnecessarily. We've always clung together against the larger clans of our kingdom when they threatened to take our lands. That's how feudalism became so unprofitable amongst ourselves, why we no longer live that way.

"The Dumnonians, with their strong king, forced us to keep their peace. In our lifetime, the only fighting we have known is the odd border skirmish with them.

'If we return, the feudalism will start again, just as in our grandfathers' time. We'd be our own worst enemies. We, from the small communities, have already lost many men and before we are through with this new undertaking, there will be more dead. How shall we protect ourselves back home with greatly diminished numbers? Will those who backed out of the invasion remember our fathers' names?

"The priesthood certainly does not care how we live back at home. To them, our lives are expendable, so long as they can fulfill their religious aims. When our lives have been forfeited, just like our fathers', there will be no one at home able to talk of our quest. Our women and children will hear only the tales told by their new overlords, for there'll be none of the warriors left who went on this fool's errand.

"In the spring when the king invades, the original aim of the conquest will most likely be successful, completely overshadowing our own failure: our brave dead will have no place next to the king's heroes."

"They will be honoured in Valhalla," said Aldred.

Cuthbert made no answer, merely gazing, unseeing, into the trees and ferns. Aldred sighed, knowing Cuthbert did not have the religion in his heart—neither did he.

"Cuthbert, you're right. But I ask you, honestly, what can we do? Should we have turned around and gone back with Dunstan, as he wished us to?" He paused, allowing Cuthbert time to reply. When none came, Aldred tried again, "If I had complied with Dunstan's wishes, the deaths of our fathers, Edgar and Lambert would have been meaningless. Besides, I asked Dunstan to take control of the village back home. If I should die on this mission, he will continue as overlord in our community. Any of you who return will retain your status under his lordship."

This was welcome news to Cuthbert: Dunstan was much respected, even by the big clans, and had been a good friend of Leofstan. It comforted the young warrior to think of his mother, sister and younger brothers secure under Dunstan's protection. He was certainly no tyrant.

CHAPTER EIGHT

The Celtic peasants crawled cautiously into position among the ferns. To their rear, the Dumnonian warriors were hidden, the idea being for the peasants to expose their position in order to tempt the Saxons into the foliage after them.

The advancing Saxon army could be heard in the distance, for they made no attempt to quiet their noisy chatter.

Arrows were once again strung and ready to be unleashed when the word was given. Caradoc had been quite clear on what would happen if any man fired in advance of the order.

***

Unaware of enemy eyes peering out at them, the first of the Saxons passed by, looking tired and bedraggled. After walking most of the morning, their alertness to any danger lurking in the forest had diminished; they seemed more concerned with staying awake. Intermingled with them were their pagan priests, the resolute of the army, the stimulant which drove them on. It was an untidy line, with the men walking in scattered groups as they chatted.

A shout rang out as the last of the Saxon line passed the area where the peasants lay hidden, soon followed by the deadly sound of shafts cutting through the air. A hail of arrows stabbed wickedly into the Saxons caught in the crossfire.

Hearing the commotion, Cuthbert and Aldred looked back and saw a horrifying sight. Men were rolling in the dirt with arrows protruding from them; their screams tore through the forest.

Some two hundred Dumnonians had concentrated their attack on a group of about twenty-five Saxons with devastating effect: among the injured were men with six or seven arrows in their bodies.

Aldred's clan, walking just in front of the group which was attacked, had escaped injury.

Turnstan's eyes widened in panic as he yelled, "Get down, get down!" He flung himself foreword and roughly knocked Aldred and Cuthbert to the ground. It was not a second too soon. The same terrifying whipping of air was heard again as a second volley of arrows shot above them. A few more screams rang out from men who failed to duck in time, and the attackers broke their cover among the ferns flanking the path to run parallel with the next enemy group up the line.

Aldred's men had passed through the terror almost unscathed. Only Rhinehold had been hit in the shoulder.

Turnstan anxiously surveyed the trees to see if anyone was still lurking there. "Watch the trees, for from such hideouts, we could be picked off with ease." Reassured that no one remained, Turnstan reasoned that if his countrymen advanced into the forest, those same trees might easily trap the ambusher.

Ahead of the column could be heard the various orders being shouted by different chieftains, while the Saxons in the rear kept their heads down. After a short time, a semblance of order came about and those up ahead began to fan out into the forest with the aim of encircling the peasant Dumnonians, who were still making sporadic attacks. Their efforts had not progressed far when suddenly, hidden Dumnonian warriors began standing up from the foliage all around the Saxon relief section and the area became a seething mass of close combat. The surprised Saxons were outnumbered three to one and their puny resistance was futile against the Celtic swords, which cut them down mercilessly. Soon, all the Saxon forces, alarmed at the fellow countryman's plight, began rushing into the forest to help them.

The peasant archers quickly backed off deeper into the foliage to allow the warriors to fight.

Aldred held up his sword and screamed, "Woden be with you!" While all around him, men charged into the forest.

Turnstan made contact immediately, smashing his sword into the ribs of a Dumnonian and almost cutting him in two.

Cuthbert stopped an overhead blow with his shield, while ramming the blade of his sword right through his assailant's stomach. Then came a chilling, high-pitched scream from the Celt as the sword was pulled free.

The sound of retreat was heard—the horns blasted out from among the trees and instantly, Dumnonians withdrew from the fight in a skilled and orderly manner.

The Saxon priests began shouting out to their warriors not to follow the retreating enemy into their dark sanctuary; the main concern of the mission was still to destroy the Christian monastery.

All around was the hideous aftermath of hand-to-hand fighting. Wounded men groaned where they had been stricken, pitiful in their new, agonized world among the blood-stained ferns, no longer caring about the cause they had been enticed into supporting. All they knew now was the pain—the pain of death.

The priests tried to persuade most of the wounded to accept a swift and merciful end, but many of the chieftains refused to listen to the holy men and began shouting back in rage at what they thought was callous advice. Hacking down branches from the surrounding trees, the warriors began to assemble wooden stretchers in angry defiance of the priesthood.

At the High Priest's urging, the rest of the holy men refrained from showing their impatience and set themselves to the task of helping the wounded. It was a successful attempt to bridge the rift that suddenly formed between them, for the holy order knew it would not do to be arguing with the chieftains at this stage of the mission. Unrest was becoming all too apparent among the army, and if morale went on weakening, the priesthood would be unable to control the warriors without their chieftains' confidence.

Once again, Caradoc had gained a morale victory over the Saxons. This battle had been smaller than the first with fewer deaths, but psychologically, he had once again hit the Saxon invaders and unbalanced their inner confidence. His peasants continued to take shots at the Saxons: as the invaders proceeded with their march after the battle, they were harassed by sporadic little attacks from the archers. Again, larger numbers of men at the head of the Saxon line fanned out into the woods to try and cut the attackers off. The Saxon relief forces were larger now and much more cautious in checking for counter-ambushes. Time and again, the army would be halted, just to drive off a force of thirty or so men, with large groups going into the forest to act as flankers so the main force could move unhampered.

These groups began to take the brunt of the attacks, losing many men in order to defend the column. Not only were they vulnerable to manned ambushes; a wrong move could trigger a crude booby trap. Branches with spikes attached would swing up out of the foliage to impale an unsuspecting victim. These flanking duties were done in shifts, so the losses were spread among the different clans. Each group began to look upon the flank duty with dread.

When night came, the Saxons' fear was intensified by what the gloom held beyond the torchlight and campfires. The dancing fires lit up the long pathway, where they had halted for the night. Nobody slept; all were peering into the blackness beyond the few trees illuminated by the orange flames. No stars twinkled above them, for they were blocked out by the fire glow reflecting on the thick ceiling of leaves and branches overhead.

"This waiting game is utter torment," cursed Sighelme.

"Do you think there will be more attacks during the night, Master?" Wilfred scratched the side of his cheek.

"Be assured, Wilfred, and keep down."

At around midnight, the first Celtic arrow shot through the darkness to strike a Saxon down. All watched in horror as the wretched man tried in vain to pull the arrow from his back, he gave one terrified yell and then, as a second arrow went through his throat, let out a final gurgle—choking on his blood as he fell to the forest floor.

Wilfred was about to go to his aid, but Sighelme's arm came across and blocked him. "No, Wilfred. There is nothing that can be done for him and you will become another target."

It was only the first of many similar incidents during the night. The firelight made it possible for the Dumnonians to single out individual targets and the Saxon army lost seventeen warriors in this way. During the day, they had lost the better part of a hundred men, whereas in return, they had managed only a few kills. It was the small attacks that unnerved them: the enemy they could not see. Under such conditions, everyone was becoming edgy and rumors spread along the line that the dawn would bring a fresh onslaught.

At dawn, the Saxons hurriedly began to brace themselves in anticipation of an attack; but none came. Half the army stood guard, while the rest packed what little they carried. The morning dew clung to them, dampening clothes and greasy hair.

The shivering men pressed forward through the forest mists, stretching their cold, stiff limbs; jumping up and down to try and get their blood circulating.

Once again, large groups went out into the ferns to flank the main force on the forest pathway, and Aldred and his men had joined with another band to form such a group, about fifteen strong.

The flankers' task was a demanding one, relished by nobody: they had never before encountered such a form of fighting and it sapped their morale. Their minds dwelled on the thought of sudden death, against which they had no defense. Eyes peered into the foliage; broken branches played tricks on nervous individuals who would raise false alarms. Men would freeze or drop to the ground and lie tense and nervous until receiving the all-clear signal. Then they would reluctantly haul themselves to their feet and gingerly set forth once more.

At midday, Aldred's party was glad to be relieved by a fresh group—for whom the anxiety was about to begin—and by late afternoon, they had left the forest without a single incident that day. Ahead stretched another expanse of moorland and, despite feeling tired and worn, the Saxons wished to start ascending into it without a moment's rest. All had a strong desire to put as much distance as possible between themselves and the forest.

Once the army was well into the open ground, horsemen went out to patrol along the flanks. Some time before sunset, in order to allow the warriors to use the remaining daylight for setting up camp, the priesthood called a halt to the day's march.

Out on the open moorlands, the claustrophobic darkness bore down on the Saxon warriors, engulfing them with a dreadful sense of doom. Fear was beginning to take its toll on their courage. It was as though the land was about to swallow them up, leaving their insignificant bones to the windswept hills.

"Do you think we will reach this monastery, Aldred?" asked Cuthbert, and all eyes turned to him, the leader of the group, for an answer.

The young chieftain was all too conscious of it. The blind confidence apparent in those eyes unnerved him.

"I think we shall," he replied, displaying at least an outward enthusiasm, so as not to diminish still further their already low morale.

Sighleme seemed to see beyond Aldred's answer, but kept quiet. He knew when his cousin had doubts. Perhaps in the morning they'd be able to confide in each other, away from the rest of the band.

Aldred withdrew into his personal thoughts, worrying as he stared into the flames, and thinking, *If only they knew how afraid I really am for their lives.* He allowed his mind to wander over the last few days: how optimistic they had all been about the success of their invasion, yet now, just four days later, all their illusions had been swept away by a few Dumnonian warriors and an army of desperate peasants.

For a while, Aldred pondered on the enemy leader, Caradoc. The young Saxon could not help feeling a certain admiration for the Gwentman's constructiveness. Looking up from the fire and at his men, he said, "This foe has harassed and quickly worn down the fighting efficiency and morale of our army. With two of the three separate invading armies now out of the conflict, perhaps Caradoc will prepare to meet the remnant once again."

"If so, Aldred," began Cuthbert. "I'm sure we will meet a far greater number of Dumnonians than at that first battle by the river." It was also his conviction that the stubborn pride, so characteristic of many of his fellow high-ranking Saxons as well as himself, would cost them dear in the future—if indeed, it had not already.

" We view the outcome of the quest quite differently from the priesthood," added Rhinehold.

"It was their fear of the Christian faith which gave them the strongest desire to motivate our warriors by whatever means they could find." Aldred looked back into the fire and shook his head. "They tricked, twisted and deceived, playing on a warrior's sense of honor. Any method that presented itself to further their ambitions has been exploited to the full."

There were murmurs of agreement, but they all felt compelled to gain some honor for the deaths of their clansmen.

CHAPTER NINE

Just half a day's march to the west of the Saxon encampment lay the Christian monastery, on which the remnant of the Saxon invasion force now focused all ambition of victory.

In bygone days, the monastery had been the villa of a rich Roman colonial merchant. Unlike many of the Roman buildings, it had been to some extent cared for, particularly the wide area of ground enclosed by its walls. A chapel had been built within the walls and the villa itself was used for the monks' living quarters.

These stout-hearted and resolute Christian monks happily farmed the surrounding lands, cared for the sick and sent out missionaries to the pagan Saxon lands in the east.

But the arrival of Caradoc and his army had completely shattered this tranquil lifestyle. The Gwentman employed his followers in the task of strengthening the monastery's fortifications in the event of it being besieged by the Saxons, telling the head monk it was a secondary precaution in case his forces were defeated by the Saxons in the forthcoming battle. If such was the case, then the survivors could, as a last resort, make their way back to the monastery to defend its walls.

Under the clear, starry night, over a thousand of the armed refugees lay sprawled within the monastery's walls. Feeding them all was a growing problem, especially as their numbers increased every day. Caradoc had encouraged them all to share whatever food they had and they had complied as best they might, but still the difficulty remained. Hunting parties were out at all times of the day and night, augmented by rabbitting, falconry and fishing. The women and children picked all the edible berries they could find but, as hard as the Dumnonian horde tried, they could not adequately sustain themselves and the first signs of starvation were becoming apparent.

Seeing their plight, the monks used up all their own food stocks to help out and worked their way around the campfires distributing the big black pots of steaming hot stew: these were suspended from poles resting on the shoulders of two men, while a third measured out a portion to each person.

Caradoc was inside the villa conversing with the head monk about the increasing number of Dumnonians and their chances of repelling the Saxon invaders. They were in complete privacy and Caradoc surveyed the bleak and gloomy surroundings as he and the monk entered the make-do sanctuary. The only light came from a solitary torch on the wall. A bed was lying alongside the wall opposite the door, above which hung a crucifix. To the right were a desk and a chair below the window, the shutters of which were closed. The noise of the refugee army could still be heard from outside, which pleased Caradoc, for their natterings somewhat subdued the effects of gloom within the room.

"So, you say that the monastery will not be used as a fortress if you can beat the Saxon army on the moors tomorrow?" asked Brother Morton. His voice was soft and very matter-of-fact.

The chieftain smiled at him. For all his warrior aloofness, Caradoc felt himself warming to the priest's gentle, but clear and precise voice. He felt an internal swelling of his Christian belief, which suddenly, had become more prominent than anything he had regarded as important to his mortal existence—he was afraid. His eyes then softened as he looked to the old man who had been waiting patiently for a reply.

"That is correct, Brother Morton, we hope to defeat the pagan army before they get to the monastery. Victory is within our grasp, of that we are sure—our preparations for defending the monastery are only a secondary precaution."

"You are wise in your planning, Caradoc, and I compliment you. You have clearly done your best for us here and we thank you most sincerely. Yet still the possibility of the Saxons defeating your army on the moors, then laying siege to this monastery, is a very real one—would you not agree?" Brother Morton clasped his hands in meditation and began slowly to pace up and down in front of him.

"It's possible, certainly, but laying siege to this monastery does not necessarily mean it will fall. Tomorrow morning, when we shall rally to face the Saxons, we are also expecting a large force of reinforcements led by a man named Gryffith." Caradoc's confidence was growing all the time, as was the fighting force.

"I have heard of this man and with his numbers added to our own increased forces, we shall match the Saxon warrior for warrior. And if you include all the refugees, our army will face theirs with a three to one advantage."

Caradoc smiled as the priest became optimistic. "Besides, the men you have seen within the walls of your sanctuary are scarcely half the actual forces that will meet the enemy. Many of our number have been trailing the Saxons since they left the forest. These men are commanded by a trusted friend called Rhese, and he has good fighting forces all around the enemy."

Brother Morton reassured Caradoc, "I do honestly believe our Lord is firmly behind us and tomorrow, we will rout the Saxons. God is always with us,

Caradoc." The implied rebuke was accompanied by a smile.

Caradoc accepted it, saying, "Indeed he is, Brother Morton. May the Lord and yourself forgive my bad words?"

"I am sure our Lord does, Caradoc, and I most certainly do."

The old wise warrior gratefully nodded his compliance and decided to confine more in the priest. "With the increase among our warriors and peasants since the battle at the riverbank, I'm hoping we might be able to trick the Saxons into underestimating our numbers yet again. Careful planning will be needed if we are to take the fullest advantage of our superior numbers."

Brother Morton walked forward—his hand held before him with his fingers clasped in his excited emphasis. "Just outside the monastery is a gully, through which any traveler from the east would have to pass."

Caradoc nodded and with a big, beaming smile said, "It is a prime spot and I will make our attack there."

Stepping towards the chieftain, the old priest put his hand upon Caradoc's shoulder as if to reassure him. "For tonight, you shall have your sleeping quarters here. You need to be well rested before tomorrow's events."

With promises of bidding one another farewell in the morning, the two men parted. The old priest bowed his head in acknowledgement as he closed the door behind him.

The decision made, his thoughts became clouded by tiredness, which swept over him. As he lay down to allow sleep to take over, the last thing he heard was the sound of the peasants chattering as they moved about in the starlit night.

CHAPTER TEN

The morning mist, coupled with the smoke of the last embers of dying campfires, lay thickly upon the sleeping Saxons. Here and there, men stumbled about, rudely nudging those still asleep. Gradually, the shivering warriors began to rise, cursing as they stretched their limbs uncomfortably inside their damp garments. Teeth chattered and dew settled on eyebrows and ran down foreheads from the crown. Dirty fingers pushed aside matted, greasy locks and then rubbed sleepy eyes. The air was heavy with the pungent smell of body odor. Distant shouts of command came from the unseen chieftains, their voices drifting through the mist like troubled ghosts.

Mobilisation was quick, but this was only because neither warrior nor chieftain carried much more than his weaponry. Food for the journey consisted of the previous night's leftovers—cold mutton, which would have to be consumed on the move.

The Saxon priesthood, keen to get on with the final stages of the journey, had no wish to wait for the mist to clear, but Arfast tried his best to persuade them to anyway. He knew the dangers of walking on high ground under such conditions, but the old High Priest's reply to his worries was simply to have faith in Woden's guidance.

Rhinehold rubbed the soft, thin fluff that clung to his chin and along his jaw like a ginger moss. He nursed a slight inferiority complex about his slow growth of facial hair, a feeling not helped by his colleagues:

"I see Rhinehold's still tending that dead weasel he has fixed to his chin," mocked Turnstan.

Rhinehold's reaction was brief and to the point, "I'm in no mood for your foolery, you uncouth oaf."

"Well," added Turnstan. "I've seen more hair on a raspberry."

"Well you must eat some very hairy raspberries," spat Rhinehold.

There was a chorus of chuckling and the counter-insults had the desired effect of drawing in Wilfred, Sighelme and, for once, the usually inhibited Cuthbert. All three jeered and egged the brothers on in the hope of being entertained. Turnstan did not need much encouragement and instantly set about attacking Rhinehold's personality. Men from other clans who were within earshot, moved closer to listen. Over the past two days, all the Saxon men travelling near Aldred's small band had become familiar with the comical bickerings of Turnstan and Rhinehold.

Hearing his two men beginning to argue, Aldred smiled, but it was only a brief acknowledgement of his approval. Now he could fall back a few paces to be alone with himself and think, although this did him little good, as he knew all too well. Once again, his mind wandered into the future, wondering about his men's destiny, worrying over what would happen if their invasion achieved absolutely nothing. Such thoughts as these had been plaguing him ever since his conversation in the forest with Cuthbert.

Once again, he surveyed his fellow countrymen. All, including himself, were marching without question, further into the forbidding lands of the accursed Dumonian, southwest Celts, relying upon the Saxon priesthood to give them all some meaning of victory to take home with them. If such could be achieved, and quickly, then perhaps the king would lift his alienation of them for going against him. After all, he could hardly refuse to recognise the priesthood's success. That would only serve to divide his fragile kingdom's structure and allow the Angle tribes of Mercia a chance to exercise their own authority upon the West Saxon lands.

He presumed none of the invaders had tried to predict the outcome, or had even bothered to think about future engagements with the enemy. There was no longer any enthusiasm for the task ahead of them: it had simply been reduced to something that had to be done to which they were all committed. This campaign had provided many of them with their first battle, yet the stories told at feasts about skilled and valiant warriors had hardly prepared the more naïve and younger men for fighting. Now they had all witnessed fear and none of them were ashamed to admit it. In many ways, fear had been one of their assets, for it had brought them closer together as a people. All had seen friends butchered; all shared the brunt of grief among the Saxons.

The Dumnonians had suffered even more, and in tragic circumstances too, but they also had victories to boost their morale, enhanced by a fire of determination and faith in their leader, Caradoc.

***

At the same time the Saxons were striking camp, Caradoc was leading his Dumonian refugee remnant to the intended valley of attack, joining a force of around a thousand who had camped close by overnight.

Gryffith, the newly arrived chieftain, was present with an impressive force of warriors.

"So you will attack from one side of the gully and I shall come from the other." The young chieftain looked along the gully and pushed his fingers through his long, matted hair. He turned back to Caradoc and his eyes narrowed as though envious of the older man. There was also a touch of resentment too.

Caradoc, for his part, deduced this but said nothing. He smiled before saying, "That is my plan, Gryffith." Then, as though cautious of causing offence, he asked, "What do you think?"

The young man arrogantly nodded his approval before leaving for there was barely time for the Dumnonians to prepare themselves as the Saxons had come into view. All their efforts were then dedicated to hiding their force from the small Saxon patrols scouting ahead. However, despite such attempts at concealment, the Saxon scouts did report back to the main column about the Dumnonians' patrol movements.

***

Arfast immediately halted the column. The old High Priest hobbled alongside the supreme chieftain's horse and looked up at him. "What are you doing, Arfast?" he asked impatiently. "Why have we stopped?"

"I want to warn the men to prepare for an attack while going through the valley," answered Arfast.

"You could have done that while we were still on the move," grumbled the holy man.

"But I must make sure they are all aware and ready in such an event," said Arfast through clenched teeth. "I need to have complete confidence in my men when

I walk into battle. Do you understand that, most gracious servant of Woden?"

"Yes," replied the priest more softly, backing away from the mounted leader. "Yes, of course I do, Arfast. Please continue."

Arfast dug his dangling heels into his horse's side and cantered down the line shouting at his men, telling them of the suspected trouble ahead.

Swords were drawn and shields, formerly fastened to men's backs, were now firmly attached to forearms for defence against arrows.

Anguish molded its distraught pattern on the Saxon faces as they moved cautiously ahead. The tops of their hands and foreheads began to perspire, as though the humidity left by the early morning fog had suddenly intensified.

***

To the Dumnonians watching, it was clear their Saxon foe had developed a shrewder sense of safety. The Teutonic invaders would not be so easily tricked this time and, moreover, the Saxon army was obviously prepared to meet Caradoc's at a geographic disadvantage.

Brother Morton crawled next to the Gwentman and peered over a boulder down into the valley at the approaching pagans. "They are all holding their shields as though ready for our archers," he observed.

"Yes," agreed Caradoc. "They know there's trouble waiting."

"Does that mean our forces will not be as effective as in the battle by the river?"

"This time, we shall have to be even more effective," replied Caradoc. "A performance like the river battle would not be enough to save the monastery from destruction. Remember, we still had to retreat under the cover of darkness, but here, there can be no retreat whatsoever."

"But what tricks do you have lined up for them?" pursued the priest.

"None," said Caradoc. "Apart from having greater numbers now and the terrain being to our advantage, our forces have no tricks for gaining total victory, except by hard and determined fighting."

Somewhat skeptically, the old priest asked, "Do you really think we have the capability to defeat these Saxons now?"

"Trust in the Lord," reprimanded Caradoc, smiling, and with that, the burly chieftain got up and walked away, denying the old priest any opportunity for riposte. Not that Brother Morton could, anyway. He was left quite speechless by the swift rebuke and secretly pleased that Caradoc was able to show him the Lord's lesson in humility.

"They are coming up the gully!" yelled Caradoc to his sub chieftains.

The order was passed around for the Dumnonians to prepare. Peasants strung their arrows and warriors mounted horses in readiness for the attack about to begin. Cautiously, the fighters moved to the summit of the slope.

Caradoc looked to the old priest. "I hope Gryffith is doing likewise on the other side of the gully."

"If he is, we should be most effective." Brother Morton's adrenaline was rushing through his body—exciting him as the thick silence all around waited for the word to attack.

***

Down in the valley when the Saxons heard the sounds of horns blasting from the scarps on either side, they stopped immediately to peer up the rocky slopes for any signs of their enemy. The blue sky was suddenly filled with raining shafts, whistling through the air and descending upon them. Swiftly, they held their shields aloft in an effort to protect themselves.

Aldred and his men were caught in the area where the main concentration of arrows fell, but none were injured, although Wilfred had come close. Seeing a man hit in the chest a few feet from where he crouched, the youth immediately dropped his shield guard to crawl over to the wounded man's aid.

"No, Wilfred!" scolded Sighelme, boiling with rage at the youth's folly.

Quickly, Wilfred raised his shield again, just in time to deflect an arrow. Two more hit the warrior whom he'd been trying to reach, thus putting the wretched man beyond the aid of anyone.

During this sustained arrow attack, there were few casualties and fewer deaths; the Saxons being widely scattered, the Dumnonians could not concentrate their shooting on specific groups.

All looked up in fearful wonder when they heard a distant enemy horseman shout out and raise his sword. All assumed correctly the man was Caradoc— the enemy chieftain who had caused them so much unexpected trouble.

The Celtic chieftain screamed out to his mounted warriors, kicked his horse and led the charge of almost six hundred down from the northern slope.

Although being spread out over a wide area made the Saxons less vulnerable to the arrows, it also put them in extreme danger from the horsemen who were galloping down the scarp of the moors—hooves thundering through the ground and about to descend upon them.

Arfast was quick to act. "All men with horses mount up and advance to the front, fast!" he bellowed. Like faint echoes, his words could be heard all around as the command was repeated and Saxons on horseback began to gather around Arfast, awaiting the order to charge.

"Attack!" he screamed and about two-thirds of the mounted Saxon horde surged forward. The rest had still not managed to rally to the call and it was as Saxons on foot began to run around in a desperate attempt to form a line of defense against the Dumnonians, the remaining Saxon horsemen began galloping out in the wake of their leader.

Caradoc had time to register surprise as he saw Arfast's mounted warriors flow together as if from nowhere, and advance to meet him, and then the contact was made with a sustained clash of steel, screaming of men and neighing of horses.

This was a bloody duel, with steel piercing soft flesh and laying bare the gaping wounds of stunned men. Horses reared, throwing their burdens to the ground, where they were trampled in the melee. Raging screams and scathing curses were abundant amid the clash of metal and wooden shields.

Arfast fought defiantly, shouting reassurance to his men, constantly coaxing and encouraging them. Many Dumnonians met their fate at his hands, but his skill with the sword proved to be no deterrent. More men came at him, as though drawn by some uncanny force. Uttering oaths, he lashed out at them, pulling his legs tighter into his horse's sides. Some of his own men struggled desperately to come to his aid, seeing that he was being surrounded and cut off from support. The Celtic pack smothered and engulfed him like a tide rolling up the sands and as they dispersed, Arfast was laying dead upon the blood-soaked turf. No Saxon saw him meet his fate—they only heard him spitting out curses in a vile rage, the clanging of his sword, then a brief silence.

***

Caradoc and a small number of his Dumnonians had managed to smash their way through the Saxon charge, and they now continued onwards towards the enemy footmen, who had formed a line of defense. The Dumnonian charge had lost momentum; no longer were they inspired by a violent passion for fighting. They had all been shocked by the interception of the Saxon horsemen and their expectations of what the charge would achieve had suddenly lessened.

Just before Caradoc's scattered remnants engaged in their second action, they met with the footmen's deterrent. As they were about to clash, spears, axes and even rocks fell upon them, knocking many from their horses. Saxon warriors stepped aside from the Dumnonian horsemen's lances and many skillfully unhorsed the Celts and slew them before they could recover from their fall.

The shocked Dumnonians changed course and retreated sideways, back up the slope. The remainder of their men on horseback, who still fought hard in the first clash, began to disengage from the contest.

***

Aldred looked to his clansmen. "Arfast's charge has worked, although at the cost of his own life."

"Yes," agreed Sighelme. "The few Celts who had managed to break the lines have easily been repelled by us footmen."

"There will be more yet to come," Cuthbert added nervously.

Caradoc now broke off the action abruptly to reconsider his strategy. Underestimating the Saxons had been a grave error, for his pagan foe had caught him out in a way similar to his own trick previously. The Celtic chieftain quickly put the failed assault out of his mind and set to gathering his forces for another attack. This time, there would be a slower and more cautious approach to the enemy. On either side of the moor slopes, the Dumnonian foot warriors formed defensive lines with the peasants standing behind them, bows and arrows ready in hand. Slowly, the Christian forces descended the hill.

***

"They are coming at us from both sides!" shouted Turnstan.

They could see all too well what the Dumnonians were hoping to do; while they fought against the warriors, the peasants would easily pick them off. Again, it was a strategy used in the last battle to aid an orderly Celtic withdrawal from the action, but this time, it would be a form of attack.

Hastily, the Saxons formed a crude line of defense, much the same as the Dumnonians'. All Saxon horsemen dismounted so as not to present themselves as targets, and behind the Saxon wall stood more warriors, spears clasped ready to throw at those wretched peasants who killed at a long distance and then ran like rabbits before any Saxon could avenge his countrymen's death. Curse the peasants and their bows: this time it would be different.

The Saxons split into two groups to fight the Dumnonians on either side of the valley. They did not wait for the action to come to them at the bottom of the slopes, preferring instead to ascend and fight on the scarps, where they had a clear view of their enemy.

As the congested lines of the armies met on both sides of the valley, the Saxons at the rear began to throw rocks at the Dumnonian peasants and a few spears found their targets. Such action as this deterred the peasant archers.

"Be ready," warned Aldred, looking behind to his clansmen. "Stick together and watch one another's backs."

Putting up his shield to fend off his assailant's sword, Cuthbert stabbed forward with his own blade and felt it dig into the Dumnonian's shield. For a moment, the two men grappled together with the way of unseasoned fighting men, but before either of them could separate from their locked combat, the Dumnonian was killed by Wilfred, who slit the enemy's throat with his scarmasax.

Only a few feet away, Aldred made a kill by kicking his opponent's legs out from under him. Before the stunned foe could gather his confused wits, it was too late: Aldred's sword had come smashing down upon his skull.

Turnstan swung his sword with a skill unmatched by any of the warriors around him. Many of the Dumnonians would not attempt to challenge him on their own. In groups of two or three they tried, but Rhinehold was never far from his brother's side. When fighting, the two of them always liked to stand back-to-back, both having an unspoken confidence in each other's fighting ability.

The whole band fought well and bravely, nurturing a ruthless efficiency in battle, with someone always close by to help when an opponent looked to be gaining the upper hand. They all kept calm when keeping watch over enemy moves, but could act quickly when they saw an opening.

'Stabber.' The most common shout for assistance among Aldred's men, was answered by Wilfred. The youth would dart about looking for opportunities to attack the enemy fighting his comrades. He was the spare man of the group, always searching to assist, yet if ever he was challenged directly by a Dumnonian, someone always came to his aid quickly—usually Sighelme.

On both sides of the valley, the Dumnonians were beginning to fall back. This was no retreat in blind panic; in fact, it was quite orderly. The Saxons who relentlessly pushed the Dumnonians further up the scarps of the moors were paying heavily.

***

On the side of the valley from where Aldred's men fought, the newcomer, Gryffith, was to lead the mounted charge while Caradoc took command opposite. Yet again, the Saxon army had been prepared for such a move, keeping their own horsemen back in reserve among the warriors. who were throwing spears and stones at the enemy peasants.

Caradoc peered down the hill to where, on the other side of the battling horde, he could see Saxon horsemen preparing for his next attack. Over on the other side, a similar reception was awaiting Gryffith. At a slow trot, he led his horsemen forward, keeping them compact and in line, but as they neared the enemy position, they suddenly increased speed to a charging gallop. Before Caradoc's formation could break up, losing the effectiveness of sudden impact upon the enemy, contact had been made.

The Dumnonian foot warriors and the peasants had quickly fled to the side, leaving their opponents standing in the path of the charging horsemen. Many of the Saxon warriors met their fate as Caradoc and his men smashed through their, now futile, line of defense. The helpless footmen made vain attempts to unhorse the enemy as the charge ruthlessly descended upon them and here and there, a few Celtic horsemen did fall; but these small achievements made little difference to the attack in general. Within the confused terror that followed, the Saxons were impaled, trampled and hacked in the ferocious charge.

Once the Dumnonians had dealt with these first unprepared warriors, they met a new challenge—this time, on horseback, like themselves.

Again, Caradoc found his plans impeded by Saxon horsemen, for his own men had emerged from the first contact in sporadic groups, making them easy targets.

Soon, the air was again filled with the clanging of steel against steel and the bashing of metal on wood amid the battle raging all around, coupled with the constant terrified screams of dying men.

***

On the southern valley scarp, where Gryffith had led a Dumnonian charge, fate had favored the Saxons on foot. Among them, Aldred and his clansmen maintained determined efforts in the fighting and the battle was running quite differently from Caradoc's side. The Saxon horsemen had been allowed through, thus preventing the onslaught threatened by the Dumnonian charge. All the Saxon footmen rushed forward to mingle with the fighting horsemen and in such cramped conditions, it was quite impossible to swing a sword.

Cuthbert presented himself as a target for a Celtic horseman whose interest seemed momentarily centered more on his colleagues' misfortunes. Lazily stabbing his sword downward and somewhat awkwardly at the irritating Saxon, it dug harmlessly into the wood of Cuthbert's shield. The young Saxon then lunged forward with his own sword, upwards into the Celt's stomach, through his diaphragm and into his chest cavity, the Dumnonian stiffened, screamed, went limp and slid off his horse. Only when the corpse lay still on the earth did the Saxon withdraw his blade, gritting his teeth sadistically as he slid the bloodstained implement free.

***

Great numbers of Dumnonian horsemen were wrenched from their mounts and hacked to death by the frenzied Saxon foot warriors, and soon, all the Celtic footmen had fled back up the moor in terror.

Now Gryffith signaled for his horsemen to retreat, too, hoping to regroup his scattered forces at the top of the hill. As they broke away from the battle, the Saxons eagerly filled the ground they were leaving behind.

The Dumnonian chieftain caught up with his foot warriors and peasants on the summit and found most of them quite calm after their recent terror. Some men had even started to organise small groups to prepare for the next stage of the conflict. Gryffith's arrival hastened things up. A new wall of defense was formed against the Saxons, who were now ascending the moor.

***

Among those Saxons who had fought against Gryffith, morale was high. Within a short time, the Gewisse had gained control of the entire slope, and as they moved on towards the summit, all harbored a strong conviction that soon, it would be in their hands.

On the northern slope, however, the story was very different, for there, the Saxons had been completely routed. Many fled into the valley with

Caradoc and his men in pursuit, mercilessly cutting them down. As they began to flee eastward, Saxons flung their weapons down in order to increase their speed.

***

With great difficulty, Caradoc finally managed to check his warriors from pursuing the panic-stricken Gewisse, for they had much to do in defeating the second force currently pushing Gryffith and his forces back over the southern moor.

Gathering his trusted sub commanders around him, the Gwentman began to outline his plan of attack. First were the Dumnonian horsemen, lining the bottom of the moor. Behind them, waited the foot warriors and the peasants and, on the command of Caradoc, all began to advance up the hill towards the new conflict.

***

When Aldred heard shouts of alarm among his countrymen, he turned and saw for the first time a long line of Celtic horsemen trotting up the scarp towards them. Behind them ran the foot warriors, brandishing swords and spears. The young Saxon turned back to look at Gryffith's forces in front. Beyond them, in the distance, he could see the monastery they had come so far to destroy. Its villa walls tormented him: after all their efforts, this represented a last hope of justification for their invasion. Without that solitary gain to present to Ceawlin, that he might forgive them and take them back among the West Saxon Lands, the many deaths among the Gewisse would have been pointless.

Again he surveyed the Dumnonian horsemen approaching from behind, close enough now to see their long, hanging locks thrown about their heads in weird and grotesque patterns as they bounced up and down upon the charging mounts.

Turnstan stopped alongside him, "Our horsemen are making ready to face them."

"And what of the horsemen who are still on the summit?" asked Aldred, meaning Gryffith and his men.

"They'll probably take advantage of the situation. We must repel them as best we can while what remains of our horsemen try to carve our escape route through Caradoc's forces."

Aldred frowned, then his mouth dropped open as he stared in disbelief. "So it has come to this." He was shaking his head. "No, it can't end like this."

"It must, Aldred," continued Turnstan, "We have to escape. We're fighting for survival now. There's nothing left to gain, survival is all that matters."

"Get Sighelme and the rest here now," said Aldred, but in fact, they were all fairly close, frozen at the sight of the new threat. They flocked round Aldred, anxious to hear what he had to say.

"The same rule applies now: we must stick together. Fight next to the clans with large numbers, but try to follow our horsemen through Caradoc's forces. The enemy forces on the top of the moor will be coming down to hack at our heels. As you can see, we are trapped. Our only hope is to smash a path out of this dilemma and then flee to the forest."

"Where hidden archers will be waiting to let fly against us," said Sighelme.

The thundering hooves drew nearer as the remnant of Saxon horseman moved forward and charged down the slope to meet the oncoming threat.

"I haven't got much confidence in our horsemen," added Rhinehold. "Once they break through the enemy ranks, they'll probably ride like the wind, leaving us to fend for ourselves."

"That is why we must remain right behind them," said Aldred.

At that moment, a commotion within the Saxon ranks captured their attention. It was the old High Priest, looking panic-stricken as he staggered around, calling to those near him. With outstretched hands, he implored them repeatedly, "You cannot turn back now, your goal is just over that hill," and pointing to the summit where Gryffith and his men stood, poised for a new offensive. "I beseech you all to listen to me, we must push on." He stopped and surveyed the faces staring back at him, expressionless, void of all feeling or ambition.

Suddenly, he felt afraid and turned in agitation from face to face, hoping someone would be comforting to look upon.

The sound of horses' hooves came to his ears. Looking up, he saw a warrior riding towards him, one of Arfast's men. Unlike the rest, this warrior was smiling—though that brought little comfort to the old priest. Few noticed the look of contempt in the rider's face, for all eyes were on the raised spear as it was struck into the old man's chest. He gave a wretched cry and staggered back holding the implement that protruded from his breast. He coughed up blood and sank to his knees, battling futilely to cling to his wretched life that was ebbing away from him.

None bothered to watch the old priest die—the incident being quickly dismissed for the more important matters at hand. Turning their attention back towards Caradoc's advancing columns.

To the rear, Gryffith commanded his horsemen to start walking their mounts forward down the moor. Behind, followed a line of foot warriors, with the usual disorganized rabble in the rear, armed with their bows and farming implements. Caradoc's force was set up in exactly the same way. The two armies began to close in on the trapped Saxons.

The moors were silent, save for the sound of horses' hooves. Nobody spoke or moved and the tension was ready to snap at any moment.

An angry Saxon scream for attack ripped through the silence, followed by an explosive roar of voices from both sides.

From the Saxon mass, a party of about a hundred and fifty horsemen emerged, galloping down a smooth, steep incline, grouped closely together in a long line. They hit a small part of the Dumnonian horsemen's wall, where only a futile resistance could be offered against the charge.

Celts were flung to the ground as their horses reared in panic, while others were suddenly wrenched from their beasts' backs. The Saxons ploughed straight through the first wall of defence into the second, comprising of Dumnonian foot warriors, whose resistance to the charge was even weaker than that of their horsemen. Most fled before the galloping horses. Those who did not were either trampled or hacked down.

Saxon faces grinned and eyes sparkled from their weather-beaten faces as they saw the masses of wretched peasants fleeing in panic down the moor in terror before their onslaught. They did not pursue them, but instead, galloped their mounts around in a semi-circle to attack an undefended part of the Dumnonian line from the rear, creating a new breech in their wall of defence.

Aldred and his men were among the first of the footmen to reach the confused sections of Dumnonians recently hit by the mounted attack. As quickly as possible, small Saxon bands began to percolate through the first line of the enemy, already broken by the horsemen, to the second, where the Dumnonian foot warriors were also trying to regroup after the blow delivered by Saxon horsemen.

Sighelme, his sword clasped tightly in both hands, surged forward with a fierce battle cry to strike down a Dumnonian, who had hesitantly stepped up to challenge him.

One Dumnonian let out his own defiant cry of vengeance as he moved against young Wilfred. The youth made a determined effort to stand his ground, stopping the Celt's blow with his flimsy shield, the force of which almost shattered his arm. But before he could make any further move, he was violently smashed in the face by the rim of his opponent's shield.

As the Dumnonian looked down upon the unconscious youth, raising his sword to chop the young Saxon in two, a blood-curdling scream turned his attention away. He swung his body around to face the new danger. It was Rhinehold, whose battle cry ceased as he felt the Dumnonian's sword tip cut across his breast. Dropping his sword, his legs buckled slightly as he staggered back a step; the enemy warrior had been fast, not the sort of opponent at whom to scream to warn of an attack.

Again, the Dumnonian swung his sword and, as the blade cut through the air, it made a swishing sound that ended with the smashing of Rhinehold's chin. The unfortunate Saxon was lifted off his feet by the force of the blow and fell to the ground mortally wounded, with the lower part of his face and jaw shattered. As Rhinehold's assailant turned once more towards Wilfred, it was the last action of his life, for there was Turnstan, in a fury, avenging his dead brother by chopping off the crown of the Dumnonian's head.

***

Soon, the Saxon army and Caradoc's men were intermingled. There no longer existed any formations on either side. Horsemen waded awkwardly through a sea of struggling, desperate men, who hacked away at each other in savage abandonment. Rage, curses and screams tore out from all directions as this vile entity of human filth seethed and rolled down the scarp towards the gully.

Gryffith, bringing his own men back down the moor's slope, could not attack the Saxon forces, for he would trample down as many of Caradoc's men, if not more. He halted his force and watched as though mesmerized by the ferocity of it all.

***

Wilfred, slightly concussed, was helped to his feet by Cuthbert. "Quickly, Wilfred, you must try and pull yourself together. Do you understand? You must," he said with concern.

Dazed and with Cuthbert's help, Wilfred began to descend the hill. Gradually, his senses came back to him. His top lip throbbed with pain, feeling as thick as the wooden pole of his spear.

With gritted teeth and brimming eyes, Turnstan looked at the blood on the blade of his scarmasax as he knelt beside the dead body of his brother, Rhinehold. He had taken the life of his injured brother before Rhinehold could regain consciousness and feel the agony of his wounds. He looked up to see Aldred standing by him. The young chieftain was much grieved by what he saw. No words were exchanged between them—none were needed. They clasped hands and Aldred pulled Turnstan to his feet. "We must be off," he said.

They set off down the slope with a number of other Saxon warriors who had managed to break out of the Dumnonians' trap, including Cuthbert, Wilfred and Sighelme. When they were a little way down the hill, Sighelme stopped to look back up towards the battle and was heartened to see that other Saxon bands had managed to break through the Dumnonian defenses. As his eyes followed the valley stream westward, he saw a building, far off on another distant moor.

"Aldred," he called. As the chieftain turned to him, Sighelme pointed to the far-off villa. Aldred gritted his teeth as he realized this was the coveted monastery, then tore his eyes from the sight, aware he was now as close to it as he was ever going to be.

Gradually, all the small groups of escaping Saxons began to join together in order to protect themselves against the Dumnonian horsemen who were beginning to segregate themselves from the battle, ready to pursue the enemy fragment which had managed to escape.

***

On the slope where the battle was still being fought, the remaining Gewisse warriors also began to clump together to make one final stand against the overpowering might of the Dumnonians. One by one, each resisting group of Saxons fell to the Celtic onslaught. Few survived the massacre, save those who had already escaped into the valley below by the skin of their teeth. As the Dumnonian horsemen descended the moor in pursuit, they found themselves locked in a galloping conflict with the escaping Saxon horsemen and, for a time, Caradoc's men had to dedicate themselves to dealing with their enemy counterparts.

One Saxon, knees gripped tightly to his mount, moved in alongside Caradoc's right flank, but the Gwentman deflected his blow by twisting his hip to use his further shielded side on his left, then brought his sword down upon the Saxon horse's rump, hacking into the wretched beast's flesh. Off it went at full gallop, throwing the rider sprawling along the ground. The Saxon survived the fall but foolishly tried to raise himself to his feet; Rhese was following and saw the man pull himself to his knees—but no further, for Rhese swung his sword in an underarm stroke as he passed the unwary enemy. The Saxon's head disintegrated in an explosion of blood and bone.

Only a moment later, Rhese met his own fate. Another Saxon horseman fell in alongside him and struck his horse's neck, slicing through the mane. Man and beast went sliding along the ground, Rhese still conscious and in pain. His right arm and collar bone were broken. All he could do was lie still and hope the thundering hooves would pass harmlessly by. Many a time he had been told that a horse would jump over a stricken man lying in its path.

But another Saxon galloped up and stabbed the Dumnonian in the stomach with his spear, wrenching the weapon free as he sped past and taking Rhese's innards with it. Screaming in agony, Rhese twisted and turned; his death was to be a slow and lingering one.

Soon, enough of the Saxon horsemen had been dealt with to allow the Dumnonians to turn their attention towards the men fleeing on foot. Caradoc led a group of about ten horsemen hoping to score a few kills. There were shouts of warning among the enemy bands, who stopped immediately to resist, hurling rocks and spears and succeeding in unhorsing three Dumnonians.

The latest Saxon retreat on the southern side of the valley was not a spontaneous reaction to defeat; to some degree, it had been planned, and only now was Caradoc beginning to learn this. He pulled his men back a little in order to let his numbers grow, as more of his warriors disengaged from the running conflict with the Saxon horsemen, now much reduced in number.

Hoping to launch a second and much stronger charge upon the enemy footmen, the Gwentman trotted some yards behind them, allowing his own ranks to swell; but fortune was not on his side. He caught sight of a line of Saxon warriors ahead of those he was pursuining, a large number of them on horseback. As the hundred or so Saxon footmen ran towards their rescuing countrymen, Caradoc called his men to a halt.

***

At the sight of the Saxon force ahead of them, Aldred had shouted to Turnstan with joy. A gap opened within the line, allowing the men to scramble through to relative safety.

***

The small force of Dumnonian horsemen only numbered around eighty, for the rest were up on the south slope butchering the Saxons who were still trapped.

Now a force of around three hundred escaped Saxons stood ready to face Caradoc's eighty-odd horsemen. Edging his mount a few paces forward, Caradoc stopped at the head of his men to survey the opposing force. He estimated there were at least fifty horsemen among them. As he watched, one of the enemy horsemen rode up to stand at the front of his own line. He had long, thin, fair hair, oily and matted, with an untidy red beard.

Caradoc looked into the man's light blue eyes, ice-cold and menacing. There was a suggestion of delight on the otherwise stony face. After a while, he suddenly turned to his men and ordered them, "Return to the main body up on the southern slope, where the other, less fortunate Saxons are making a last stand." He then looked back at the Saxon before him, allowing his vision to sweep about the enemy horseman. Finally, his gaze returned to the bold horseman who was before his escaping force of Saxons. "You and I will meet on another day," he grinned and nodded his head.

The Saxon nodded his head with a compliant smile and then, likewise, commanded his force to continue with the retreat eastward, back to the West Saxon lands.

The Gwentman watched them go. They had evaded death for today; but he vowed to hunt and kill the retreating remnant, all the way back to their own country if necessary. With that, he galloped after his own men, back to where the battle was still being fought.

CHAPTER ELEVEN

Although the trapped Gewisse warriors fought desperately, they could not prevent the inevitable. One by one, their little groups began to grow smaller, increasingly outnumbered. Eventually, those who were left threw down their arms in the hope of gaining mercy; only the most noble of the Saxons fought on for an honourable death—with which the Dumnonians most willingly obliged.

Of those Saxons who surrendered, about a hundred and fifty in all, most were wounded. Although many of the demoralized warriors pleaded for help, it was to no avail. The Dumnonians had their own injured to care for.

The defeated and demoralized men were herded to the summit of the moor and made to sit there throughout the night. All around them was a line of guards who wore thick woolens and cloaks to keep themselves warm against the night winds, but for the prisoners, there was no such luxury, and many of the wounded died of exposure.

Gryffith and Caradoc met each other formally for the first time that night. When the feasting was finished, they left the tent to find privacy in which to talk. Walking among the small fires on the leeward slope of the moor, they eventually found themselves upon the summit, where a strong breeze swished through their hair and fluttered cloaks about.

"So this is what is left of our pagan horde," began Gryffith. "They certainly do not look so bold now, do they? In fact, rather wretched is how I would describe them." He looked around at the huddled prisoners.

"There are many more who escaped and are trying, even now, to get back to their own territory. They must be hunted down and killed, as many of them as possible—I don't want too many getting back home. Those Saxons who decided not to come along with this lot will be even more put off from making another attempt," remarked Caradoc.

"Or inflamed into trying," answered Gryffith.

Caradoc looked at the younger man, who was lean, handsome and had smooth skin like a baby. As yet, there was not even a whisker on his chin, so young was he. Not long ago, his father had died, leaving him, the only son, to inherit all his property.

Caradoc had expected to see a young and very naïve man and on first sighting him, losing his part of the battle, he'd thought his surmise correct. Their first meeting had destroyed all such illusions. Gryffith was not in awe of his older, more mature ally at all. In fact, he seemed welcome to an opportunity to contradict Caradoc.

It was not long before Caradoc began to develop a loathing for him, because he felt inferior to the young man and realized Gryffith had designs, like himself, on claiming lands under his lordship; and whatever king came to the throne of Dumnonia, would be sure to give his consent to any who had rid the land of the Saxons.

Caradoc would naturally be included in such honours, but now, the first choice of lands would go to a Dumnonian, rather than to a man banished from his own Kingdom of Gwent.

There would be a contest between the Dumnonian and himself, of this Caradoc was sure; but for now, the most important task was to deal with the fleeing Saxons. The pagan enemy would scatter in small groups and he would need to disperse his forces to track them down.

Gryffith broke into his thoughts, saying, "I shall lead my horsemen into the forest tomorrow. A large number of my footmen are marching that way already, so I can have them all there together."

Surprised, Caradoc asked, "When did you send your footmen off to the forest?"

"During the feasting."

Caradoc made no comment—but he could not conceal the angry look on his face. He wanted to ask why he had not been informed: but couldn't, because that was exactly what Gryffith was hoping for. Caradoc knew full well what answer he would get and he was certainly not going to allow Gryffith the pleasure of giving it.

The old priest appeared then, anxious to commend young Gryffith personally for rallying to the cause of ridding the land of the hated pagan foe. Gryffith was most polite to him, saying, "It is the Lord's will; for His glory and my love of Him do I come here in defense of His own Kingdom."

"Excellent, sir, excellent," beamed the old priest, thrilled at such talk.

Gryffith went on with it; he knew what the old man liked to hear and soon learnt Caradoc's approach was not too enthusiastic to the more Godly side of the old priest's zeal. The young man was silently pleased. It was unwise to be on bad terms with the church. He made a careful mental note of the cold relationship that existed between Caradoc and the old man where their belief in God was concerned. Such knowledge might become useful.

For the priest's benefit, Gryffith now said, "Well, I think it is time for rest. I plan to leave at the break of dawn, for God's work must not be left undone." To this, the old man inclined his head in polite acknowledgement, a peaceful smile upon his face.

As Gryffith descended the moor, the priest turned to Caradoc and commented, "Such a man of spirit and holy devotion. These are the sort of men Dumnonia breeds. You mark my words, Caradoc, this young man will go far."

Once again, Caradoc stopped himself from saying what he so desired about Dumnonia's breed of men. The peasants could fight, as they had proved; but as for the nobility of the land—most had fled further west. He thought the late king was probably looking down from the heavens in disgust at the Dumnonian noblemen, if all the high-ranking men of the country behaved in such a way. It was no wonder the Saxons took more and more of Dumnonia for their own kingdom. In Caradoc's opinion, a man did not deserve to own land if he was not prepared to defend it. He himself had stood up to face the enemy and protect the land, and had strong views on what he deserved; no one was going to take that away—not even Gryffith.

Aloud, he said, "He certainly knows where to be and what to say at the right time."

The priest frowned in annoyance, but said nothing; he couldn't be sure whether the youngster was being complimented or ridiculed. But then, before he could change the subject, the Gwentman was off down the hill.

CHAPTER TWELVE

There was no longer any solid leadership to bind the remainder of the Saxon army together. As they made their way eastward, some bands ran, while others walked. When night came, there were those who chose to rest and those who continued.

Aldred and his men, walking deep into the night, came upon the very forest they had been only too glad to leave a few days before. The weary men knew they would not be observed entering the woodland during those early twilight hours of morning, whereas in the daylight, it would be all too easy for the Dumnonians to spot them. Under cover of the fading darkness, however, this small band managed to get into the forest unnoticed. For a short time, they continued walking among the dark, shadowy trees.

Hearing the sound of running water, the young chieftain called a halt. Smiling to himself contentedly, he said, "Right, we shall rest and hide here for the day and continue our journey by night."

"How will we know where we are going in this place at night?" asked Cuthbert, bemused.

"We shall follow the stream."

Turnstan and Sighelme both thought Cuthbert's question foolish. How could he be so lacking in gumption as to need to ask?

"There's bound to be more killing today," said Aldred, "for some of our men will doubtless try to come into the forest while it's light. I don't give much for their chances—the eyes of the enemy will be everywhere. From now on, we shall travel only at night."

"But we could be in this forest for days if the stream twists and turns," Cuthbert put in.

"In that case, we shall be in the forest for days," said Aldred angrily. "From now on, we must concentrate on getting back home alive." That said, his anger died and he sighed, looking down at the ground. When next he spoke, his tone was soft and conciliatory. "There is no longer any unity among the Gewisse," he said, looking up at his men. "As you know, those of us left alive are now completely routed.

"The Celts are not finished with us yet. They will hunt and kill any Saxons from here to the border. Every track and pathway, all direct routes will be watched. We are in their domain, and they have the advantage.

"My plan is to follow this stream until we reach the sea and then move eastward along the coastline. We can do all this in the dark."

Turnstan walked forward into full view of the company and held Aldred's eyes with his own as he spoke, "This is indeed a very good method of travelling unobserved. It is safer, and with the rivers and coastline to guide us, we shall eventually get out of here. My only criticism is that we shall take many days—or rather, nights—longer to get home than we did to come here and I for one, have no desire to stay in Dumnonia any longer than is necessary."

"But necessity demands careful planning from now on," cut in Aldred. "There will be plenty running straight for the border, and I don't think they will make it. They have only one thought in mind: to get out of Dumnonia as fast as possible, never mind how.

"What we must do is plan how to evade the enemy and at the same time, stay alive in order to reach home. Those who think only of getting off Dumnonian soil will stand more chance of remaining on it forever, never to return home."

He paused, surveying his band. "Right now," he said, "It's morning and for us, the day is over. I want you all to rest while I keep first watch. Sighelme, you will take the second watch when I wake you."

Acknowledgement came with a nod of tangled ginger locks and then everyone crawled gratefully under brambles where they might sleep undetected. Despite their desperate plight, sound sleep came to all of them after their long hours of fighting and travelling.

Sighelme took his watch at midday, when he awoke and found Aldred had fallen asleep at the foot of an oak tree. Such a happening was very dangerous; they might all have been murdered in their sleep. At the thought, he looked around nervously.

He allowed Aldred to sleep on unhindered, not having the heart to wake him. Establishing himself on the other side of the oak, Sighelme listened intently for sinister noises among those of the wind rustling the leaves, the stream and the cheerful chatter of the birds. On one occasion, he thought he could make out the sounds of excited human shouts far off in the distance, but they soon faded away.

Towards the end of the day, he was joined by Turnstan, Cuthbert and Wilfred. In quiet whispers so as not to awaken Aldred, the four spoke of many things concerning their predicament, but the one topic to which they kept harking back was food. What would they do for such a vital necessity on their journey? Unable to come up with any suggestions, they put the problem aside until Aldred awoke.

When he finally began to stir from his deep slumber, he heard the birds singing under the thick green canopy above. As he sat up and rubbed his eyes, the smell of his dirty garments and his sticky body odour brought him to his senses.

The Gewisse as a clan had a poor reputation for cleanliness, as had most Saxon tribes. Aldred had always been lax with his personal hygiene, even for a Gewisse, but at this moment, the young chieftain felt repulsed by his condition. After all, it was still summer and their womenfolk back home could usually nag them enough to wash a little more frequently than they had done lately.

Groaning with distaste, Aldred pulled himself to his feet, stretched out both arms and arched his back, which clicked and he gritted his teeth at the sound. It pleased the young warrior to hear his bones make such a noise.

Four bedraggled faces stared at him.

"Woden, let it not be that my face looks similar to theirs," he said jokingly.

"No, it's worse," retorted Turnstan in like mood. A broad smile spread across the young chieftain's face and upon seeing it, the rest of the group grinned happily.

Straight away, Turnstan had formed a humorous bridge with the chieftain and everybody, including Aldred, felt relieved. He had been very offhand and silent towards the clan ever since the invasion, his father's death naturally adding to this. Aldred's inheritance of the chieftainship had not been under the best of circumstances, and all were aware their situation had steadily worsened ever since.

Now, at last, he was smiling and showing signs of his father's roguish personality; perhaps it was because he was alone with the remnant of his small clan and in total command; no longer forced to follow the main army and the priests.

"The question now plaguing your minds," he declared knowingly, "is food."

"Yes," agreed Sighelme, "but your face is telling me it's no longer a problem."

"Oh, it could be. It depends on whether we can find any Dumnonians in this forest without having to stray too far from the stream. There must be plenty of paths crossing it somewhere along its route. We shall wait at such a crossing in the hope of making an ambush."

"With four of us?" exclaimed Cuthbert incredulously.

"Certainly," replied Aldred, "we'll ignore large groups, of course, but I'm sure there'll be some smaller ones wandering about. They'd probably feel quite safe too; in this forest, help would be much closer to them than the furthest sounding of a horn blast. It means we'll have to make our kill quickly, quietly and very efficiently. Then we hope they have food on them." Seeing the uncertainty beneath the haggard faces watching him, he added, "I know it's not the best of solutions. If any of you can think of another way, I'd be willing to try it if it sounds more promising."

Cuthbert, Turnstan and Sighelme looked at each other, hoping for a suggestion. As a last resort, all turned to Wilfred, but the youth shook his head, surprised they might consider an ex-slave's opinion.

"Your way is best, Aldred," sighed Sighelme.

"I want to start following the stream now, in the daylight, just until we see a trail crossing it. Then we stop and pray Woden favours our future. I am sure we all know about caution as we move," said Aldred, fixing his gaze on Wildred, so the lad understood the warning was for his benefit.

Gathering up their few possessions as quickly and quietly as possible, they set off along the stream, careful to keep well hidden from any enemy who might be on the opposite bank.

Aldred would look carefully all around him before darting forward to his next chosen point of cover and then Cuthbert would dash to the space he had abandoned, with the other men doing the same in their turn.

Remembering the crude booby traps that had been laid by the Dumnonians when first they passed through the forest, the group surveyed the undergrowth thoroughly before anybody moved across the ground.

Soon, Aldred spotted a small, muddy footpath bisecting his line of travel. Although the stream was

not in sight, it could be heard, so they concluded the
path must cross the stream, too.

When all were gathered around Aldred in amongst
the foliage, he said, "This is the place. The largest
group we shall consider attacking is three—any more
than that, we allow to pass by. Cuthbert and I will
wait on the other side of the path and if three men
appear, this is what we'll do: Cuthbert and I will take
the first; Sighelme, alone, will tackle the second, while
Turnstan and Wilfred will attack the third. If, for some
reason, I decide to call off the attack, I'll make the
appropriate signal."

"What if no Dumnonians came along the path
before nightfall?" asked Cuthbert.

"Then we fight back our hunger and move on,"
replied Aldred.

But their first enemy sighting was quite unnerving
because it was a force of around two hundred warriors
heading for the stream crossing. Aldred and Cuthbert
cautiously moved deeper into the woodland, away
from the path.

About ten peasants led the force, probably bandits
who knew the woods well. After them, forty riders
were followed by the remainder on foot. All were in
high spirits, chattering excitedly. Sighelme realized
why when he noticed a bloodstained spear over
someone's shoulder and saw three Gewisse prisoners

walking among the enemy with their hands tied behind them, hanging their heads.

"They've had good hunting," whispered Turnstan. "What do you think will happen to the prisoners?"

"I have heard these Dumnonians sometimes try to convert Saxon prisoners to Christianity before putting them to death," replied Sighelme.

With the Dumnonians gone, Aldred and Cuthbert returned to their former position and the waiting began again.

Some time later, Sighelme was the first to distinguish a man-made sound among the noises of the forest. He stiffened and alerted the rest of the group. It was coming from the direction in which the army had just marched.

"How many?" called Aldred.

"Two riders," answered Sighelme.

They all tensed, ready to spring their attack. As the first rider was about to gallop by, Aldred jumped out and swung his blade at the horse's front leg with all his strength. The wretched beast fell screaming to the ground, it's hoof severed.

The rider, thrown over the animal's head, hit the earth and began to roll, knocking Cuthbert off his feet.

Frantically kicking and pulling on the reins, the second Dumnonian tried in vain to swerve. Hitting his head on a branch, he knocked himself from his

mount as the beast veered off the path. Before he
could recover, Wilfred had dispatched him by stabbing
him in the throat.

"Don't let the horse escape," shouted Sighelme,
"it might get back to the main force and raise the
alarm."

"No, leave it," yelled Aldred, "the other man's
escaping." Aldred had expected Cuthbert to deal with
the concussed rider while he put the horse out of its
misery, but now he turned to see Cuthbert stunned
and the Celtic warrior staggering off into the forest.

"Sighelme and Turnstan, come with me. Cuthbert,
you and the boy start cutting the horse's flesh up for
food, but only as much as you can carry, then follow
us."

The Dumnonian ran through the forest with all
the energy he could muster, chased by three equally
desperate Saxons. Sighelme veered off towards the
stream, hoping to put himself between the enemy
warrior and the running water. Aldred ran on the Celt's
other side, while the heavier form of Turnstan
struggled to remain at his heels.

As trees, bushes and ferns flashed by, Aldred was
suddenly aware of their beauty and wondered why
that should come to him when he was surely about to
kill amid such splendor. He tore on, his chest
pounding more violently with every fearful stride he
took. From the corner of his eye, he saw the ginger

hair of Sighelme slightly ahead and to one side of him.

Sensing Aldred's presence, too, the Celt suddenly dropped speed and dodged sideways behind Sighelme, who pulled up as he realized the Dumnonian had outwitted him. Turnstan dived for the man's heels, pulling him off balance.

Aldred pounced on the stumbling man, bringing him down. He'd been grasping his sword by the blade for quicker running, and so was unable to use it very effectively, but a gash in the man's thigh at least prevented his escape.

Panting for breath, the three Saxons began to move in on the Dumnonian, swords in hand. To the Celt, it was Turnstan who looked the fiercest and most menacing because of his height and build, and with a final burst of defiant strength, the doomed man flicked his arm awkwardly towards him. With a loud grunt of dismay, the big Saxon dropped his sword to the ground and clutched the hilt of the knife in his stomach before falling to his knees.

With a fierce yell, Aldred brought his sword down upon the Dumnonian's skull, hitting the dead man again and again. When the young chieftain's anger was spent, he stopped and looked at the bloodstains splattering his dirty garments.

"We had best find the others," said Sighelme quietly.

Slowly, Aldred turned his head to Turnstan, who was back on his feet, with one hand clasping his wound and the other his sword. "I can still move," he said.

With a silent nod in recognition of Turnstan's pride, Aldred unsheathed his scarmasax, bent down and started to cut away the dead Dumnonian's blood-soaked clothing, which he then used to wrap tightly around Turnstan's waist.

Cuthbert arrived with Wilfred, saying with concern, "We had to leave the horse's carcass lying on the pathway."

"We'll have to go back and try to move it," replied Sighelme.

"No," said Aldred, a note of panic in his voice, "let's get out of here now, while there's still time."

Dismayed, Sighelme said, "In Woden's name, I beg you to reconsider. If any Dumnonian comes down that path before daylight, he'll see the horse and know we have passed through. They'll soon find the bodies of their warriors, too, and they'll start tracking us down. By simply removing that carcass, we can hide all signs of a fight from unsuspecting passersby."

Aldred listened to his cousin in silent rage, for he did not like his authority questioned at any time. Now, even though he knew Sighelme was right, his foolish pride would not allow him to give way in front of the men. Forgetting his earlier plans about following the river by night, he growled, "We move now."

Sighelme exchanged a look of despair with Cuthbert at this folly, but they could see that Aldred was resolute. Reluctantly, they all followed after him, Turnstan declaring defiantly his wound was not too bad.

Sighelme was highly regarded by all of them, including Aldred, whose own standing was only respected because of his father's achievements. That he had proved himself in battle was without doubt, but his arrogance and erratic behaviour had let him down on a number of occasions in the eyes of his men. He could not—would not—see that the men questioned his decisions, not out of disloyalty, but in order to find a better alternative. Leofstan had always given advice a fair hearing. If he disagreed with an alternative, he would say so without anger, which earned him the respect and love of his men. He did have a bad temper, certainly, but he seemed to know when, and when not, to use it.

CHAPTER THIRTEEN

Just before evening, ten Dumnonian horsemen came riding down the pathway where Aldred and his band had made their ambush and immediately spotted the butchered horse. A short search revealed the body of one of the two riders they had been looking for since one of the horses had found its way back to the encampment.

Two of the Dumnonians picked up the corpse and slung it across a pony's back, then one of the warriors rode back to the camp to get more men to help search for the Saxons. Meanwhile, the other nine Dumnonians followed the tracks that led into the forest and before long, they found the second body. None of them even bothered to dismount; hunting wild Saxons was the sport of the moment.

***

Caradoc and Gryffith had planned to meet at the end of the day and as Gryffith led the way into the camp, his men were impressed by the array of Saxon heads impaled on wooden stakes.

Caradoc emerged from his tent and came across to greet the young chieftain as he dismounted. "Well, what can you add to our display of heathen heads?" he asked genially.

Rudely ignoring the question, Gryffith asked, "How many did you hunt down today in this forest?"

Fury wiped the smile from Caradoc's face. "Those of us here have killed sixteen men today. More of my warriors are further afield. I expect they have made significant kills, too," he replied haughtily.

"We have twenty-two heads," said Gryffith. "Should I have my men put them up alongside yours?"

"Yes," said Caradoc quietly.

"Obviously, there are still a lot of Saxons in the forest," remarked Gryffith.

"There are a lot of outlaw bands in this forest who have sworn their allegiance to us in the hope of attaining a pardon when we have a new king. They have probably had much better hunting than us, for their knowledge of the woods is excellent," said Caradoc.

"The whole of Dumnonia is breaking up into small kingdoms now," said Gryffith. "There shall be no single Overlord any more. Whatever lands we win for ourselves will be our kingdoms. I am sure that whoever takes this forest would willingly pardon the outlaws."

Caradoc was surprised to hear of the breaking up of the great kingdom, for he'd thought the late king had established a firm unity and patriotism throughout the land.

Obviously, the landowners had become more greedy: chieftains of their own petty kingdoms would not have to pay taxes. And in the present situation, it would mean that landowners in the west, whose kingdoms had not yet been invaded, would not fight the Saxons.

"You seem disappointed, when instead of hoping to be a lord, you can now be the ruler of your very own kingdom," said Gryffith in surprise.

"Are you blind?" shouted Caradoc angrily. "Where's the sense in all those small kingdoms competing against each other? We have enough trouble keeping the Saxons at bay now; how in God's name will we continue when we are feuding with each other?"

At that moment, a horseman entered the camp. People gathered around and began to chatter excitedly. Caradoc recognised him as one of the ten men he had sent out earlier in search of the two messengers, and now he pushed his way through the crowd to stand before him.

The dead body lay across the horse in front of the rider. Caradoc grabbed it by the hair and lifted up the head in order to see the face. The neck would only yield slightly, for rigor mortis was beginning to set in. "When did you find him?" he asked.

"Just before evening, sire."

"Then his murderers cannot have gone far. You will lead me to where you found him and from there, we shall follow the heathens' tracks. I trust the rest of your party are already doing so?"

"Yes, sire, they are leaving signs for us."

Soon, Caradoc and Gryffith were galloping along the pathway, followed by twenty men apiece and eight hounds. Just one man was in front, their guide, the warrior who had brought back the body.

When they arrived at the scene of the ambush, they lit torches. Once the hounds had picked up a scent, the Dumnonians followed them, holding flaming torches against the darkness.

As they searched deeper into the forest, Gryffith began to get irritable. "Do you think this little hunt is worth the attention of so many of us?" he asked.

"Of course it is," muttered Caradoc, "but no one forced you to come along. You must understand, Gryffith, there will be no more full-scale battles with any of these heathens now. They are a spent force and have separated into individual clans. Each time we kill a group of them, a whole clan will have been completely wiped out. Any who survive and manage to escape will find themselves fighting each other for the land left empty by the clans we have massacred.

"It is essential that Dumnonia unites as a single kingdom once more so we'll be ready to meet the next invasion. There will be other attempts."

Suddenly, the dogs began barking excitedly, their masters pulling hard on their leads in order to keep them from running ahead. For a while, the Dumnonians were charged with excitement at the thought of making contact with the Saxons, but it didn't last. Soon, they heard voices in their own tongue and came upon the other nine riders from the ten sent out by Caradoc.

They'd not been wasting their time and were able to inform Caradoc that the group of Saxons they were hunting numbered five, with one of them possibly wounded.

It was Gryffith who first voiced the suspicion that the Saxons might be using the stream for guidance during the night, pointing out the enemy's tracks had run parallel with the stream ever since they had first begun to follow them.

Caradoc agreed, but said, "I'm sure we can cut through the forest and come out further upstream."

"Not during the night," protested Gryffith, "we would surely lose our way."

"A few of my men know this part of the forest very well. Even in the dark, they can steer us overland," insisted Caradoc. "If I take my men into the forest, while you continue to follow the stream, we should come out on both sides of them."

Gryffith nodded his agreement to the plan and the two groups went their separate ways.

***

When Sighelme's sharp hearing alerted him to the far off baying of the hounds, Aldred said, "They are not onto our trail," in an effort to subdue the fear rising in all of them. Sighelme suspected Aldred was trying to protect his decision not to clear the dead horse's body from the path.

As the fugitives continued along the stream, it became increasingly obvious they were indeed being followed. On they plodded, trying to think of a way out of the dilemma. The idea of leaving the stream and losing themselves in the blackness of the forest was rejected, for the hounds would sniff them out and lead the Dumnonians to them.

Aldred would only instruct them to keep on moving and it was lucky for the group that he did so, because Caradoc and his men broke out of the inky blackness and upon the stream at a point the Saxons had passed only moments earlier.

Hearing the Dumnonians, who were making no attempt to be quiet, the Saxons stopped and listened. Sensing fortune was still on their side, they wasted no time in resuming their escape attempt before the Dumnonians realised how close they had come and renewed their efforts in the right direction.

Turnstan, that huge man with a burning love and pride for his clan, was aware his wound had slowed him down so he was hindering his companions. Gradually, he dropped to the back of the line.

Since hearing the Dumnonians, they had been walking in the shallow stream, and Turnstan reasoned the hounds would now be hard-pressed to find their scent. But the enemy would not need the dogs; they would surely know if the dogs could not pick up any scent, it was because their quarry was using the stream to wash it away. If a new trail was presented for the hounds to follow, the Dumnonians could be tricked into changing their search from the river into the forest.

Without any further thought on the matter, Turnstan made for the bank. Carefully, he undid the bloodstained cloth wrapped around his waist and found the wound still bleeding. He put the palm of his hand across the wound and smeared his blood across the grass. Satisfied it would attract the hounds, he made off into the forest.

Sighelme turned just in time to see him disappear. In a strained whisper, he called after Turnstan, but to no avail. Turnstan never heard, or chose to ignore, his call.

The whole group knew why the big man had left them and Aldred said, "We must try to find him."

"He hopes to buy us time," said Sighelme. "If we bring him with us, he will soon die anyway. If we leave him, he will die fighting to the last. There will be dignity for him and meaning for us.

"I swear by my love of Woden, Aldred, that I am thinking mainly of Turnstan. What he has done is for us and we should honour him by accepting the chance he has given us."

Aldred knew Sighelme was right and it infuriated him. Once again, he stood corrected. Obstinately, he repeated, "We must save him."

Sighelme looked into his chieftain's eyes, blazing with anger, and saw the blind stubbornness. There could be no more questions on his decision.

On the point of following Aldred, the Saxons froze with fear as the barking of the hounds and harsh Gaelic shouts began to grow louder. Swallowing his foolish pride, Aldred turned again to Sighelme, saying, "We owe Turnstan much." His three remaining followers said nothing. "Let's push on if we can."

When the dogs picked up Turnstan's scent, they immediately set up a howl. Caradoc halted his men, calling back to Gryffith, "The hounds have something."

"Let them lead us to the heathen scum," roared Gryffith. He had brought a big pot of wine with him, which he now greedily emptied. He flung it aside and the sound of it smashing echoed into the night. "Death to the pagan bastards!" he yelled, brandishing his sword.

A roar of approval went up around them and Caradoc, infected by the high spirits of the warriors, yelled, "Here we come!"

One hound was held back, but the rest were released into the night. They raced off, barking loudly along Turnstan's trail. The Dumnonians followed them, guided by the single hound secured to one of their horses by a long leash. With it drawn taut, the tormented beast was up on his hind legs, chafing to be with the other hounds, who were running free.

Turnstan, well aware the hounds were onto him, stopped to make his last stand at the base of an oak tree, where his back was protected. Sword firmly clasped in both hands, he got into position on one knee, ready to deal with the first animal that emerged from the sombre blackness. His body was filled with impatience to kill and be on his way to Valhalla. Now that the final test was upon him, he felt a mixture of adrenalin fuelled by fear; he would acquit himself well in the eyes of the gods of Asgard.

The first hound came bounding through the trees, quite unimpeded by the darkness of the forest. A momentary glimpse of its white teeth against the blackness was all that a fighting man of Turnstan's ability needed. Quick as lightning, he swung his spatha at the beast's muzzle, killing it with only its high-pitched yelp echoing in the darkness. Another hound was upon him before he could wrench his sword free and its weight knocked him against the tree. With all his might, Turnstan pushed the animal away from him, taking with it a lump of his flesh. He dealt swiftly with the next dog, but then two came at him together, knocking him against the tree once more. This time, he screamed unashamedly as he felt the teeth clamping viciously into his cheek. He fell to the ground kicking and trashing as more dogs sank their teeth into him.

With an effort born of desperation, he pulled out his scarmasax and plunged it into the beast which had ripped away half his face. As it sprang back, Turnstan dragged himself upright and stabbed the dog tearing at his arm.

As more dogs fell upon him, Turnstan weakened, though even as the blood gushed from his neck, he continued to struggle, until finally, it was all over. Even then, those hounds which had survived went on with their work in a frenzy, ripping his flesh apart.

The tethered dog led the Dumnonians into the clearing, their torches clearly illuminating the bloody spectacle of four dead hounds and the body of a tall Saxon warrior. The remaining dogs were oblivious to their masters' presence and paid no heed to Caradoc when he tried to call them off.

The Gwentman was very impressed with the dead warrior's last stand. Despite being an enemy, such a man deserved honour. Caradoc had learnt to respect bravery above all things and he envied the dead man's courage.

Realising the Saxon had deliberately put himself out as bait for the dogs so the rest of his companions could escape, Caradoc said, "It's a trick."

"What do you mean?" asked Gryffith.

"He has led us off the trail of the rest of them," he explained.

"Heroics amongst heathens," sneered Gryffith.

"Yes, and you would do well never to underestimate their courage and cunning. Remember, they are good warriors."

It was a severe knock for Gryffith's youthful pride, and in front of his own men, too. For once, he was speechless and simply stared angrily at Caradoc.

The older man wished he had been a little more tactful in his reproach, for the young man's eyes blazed with hate in a look that seemed to be planning some future evil.

Calmly, the Gwentman said, "Let us return to the stream." They turned away, leaving darkness to cloak the scene of murder.

As the piteous baying of the hounds gradually died away in the distance, it was replaced by the excited howling of wolves closing in.

CHAPTER FOURTEEN

Deep into the night, the four Saxons began to jog along the river. Poor visibility made it difficult and they strained their eyes to make headway. The moon was a great help; wherever its light managed to filter through, the water reflected the brief little gleams of silver. Soon, the Dumnonians would be on their trail, they knew, for they'd heard the distant growling of the hounds as they fought with Turnstan.

The departed warrior's bravery had fired them with the determination to make good their escape. Such a noble friend should not be allowed to die in vain. If the Dumnonians should catch up with them, then they would all fight to the last.

As the sound of barking hounds began to come to them along the stream, they were filled with fear and stopped. Aldred looked at Sighelme and said, "We'll have to face them. If we continue to run, we'll be caught unprepared. I'm sure if we can trick them into thinking there are more of us than there actually are, we might beat them into a retreat and buy ourselves more time."

Sighelme's confidence in the young chieftain was renewed. Perhaps Turnstan's death had pulled him to his senses and he was thinking clearly and positively again.

"I agree, Aldred," he added cautiously, "but may I make a suggestion?"

"Yes, by all means."

"We cut down as many thin branches as possible, the thickness of a spear, sharpen their ends and place them at intervals along either side of the bank. When we begin our ambush, the Dumnonians will be unsure of our numbers, so if we ran along the bank throwing these spears from different positions, they might be confused into thinking there are more of us."

"It sounds good," agreed Aldred. "We could also try to put some weight just above the sharpened tips." Telling Wilfred and Cuthbert to begin cutting branches, Aldred began to rip off strips of his clothing and so did Sighelme. As Cuthbert and Wilfred brought them the branches, Sighelme sharpened the ends and then handed them to Aldred, who tied strips of material just above the sharpened points in order to give weight to the crudely made spears.

When about twenty had been made, Aldred said it was time to prepare for the ambush. Sighelme and Wilfred gathered up half the spears and ran across to the opposite bank. They now had five spears apiece, except for Wilfred who had six, including the one he had retained since the beginning of the invasion, and each man selected his own run; making sure he would know the way in the dark and also, where every spear was positioned.

While they waited, their nervousness grew, tormenting them with fears of hideous and painful death. They were impatient for the Dumnonians to come upon them so the fight could begin, for better or worse.

After what seemed an eternity, the Dumnonians finally came into view, their figures silhouetted by torchlight, their hounds straining ahead.

Aldred allowed the first rider to come within throwing range, then screamed as he slung the first spear. It was the signal for the other Saxons to do likewise.

Hit in the chest, Aldred's target screamed and fell from his horse into the stream, where the cold water soon brought him back to his senses. He pulled the stake from his body and made ready to stagger back alongside the others, unhindered by the attack.

Quickly, but cautiously, Aldred walked along the bank to his next throwing position, finding it easily despite the darkness, by counting his paces.

His three comrades had caused a lot of disturbance; Wilfred had caused a horse to rear with his shot, casting another frightened but uninjured Dumnonian into the stream and Sighelme, too, had hit a horse. As it reared up and threw its rider onto the bank, the Dumnonian fell close to Cuthbert, who could see by the flickering light that he was vulnerable. Dashing from his cover behind some bushes, he stabbed the man in the neck with a stake. Pulling it free, he turned and threw the bloodied weapon at the confused melee of Dumnonians, then with quick wit, he grabbed the pony's reins, unsheathed his scramasax and cut into the beast's throat. It reared and wrenched itself free, but the damage was done—the enemy would have no use of the dying mount.

Aldred, Sighelme and Wilfred were now at their second positions of attack and three more spears fell into the crowd of horsemen, one of them hitting a man in the back.

Soon, Caradoc could be heard shouting through the night and although the Saxons could not understand the Gaelic tongue, they could tell by the tone of the Gwentman's voice that the Dumnonians were beginning to panic.

Joy, triumph and a new spirit of determination were mingled in the four Saxons as they watched their hunters depart. Gathering up the remainder of their spears, they set off once more along the stream. Behind them, one Dumnonian lay dead, another was wounded with a spear in his back and a pony painfully snorted away, stressed and inconsolable in the stream.

***

When Caradoc and Gryffith reorganised themselves, they soon discovered the extent of the damage and began calling for one of their missing men.

Dismounting, the Celts began to stalk warily along either side of the bank, expecting to make contact with the enemy again, anticipating with each meticulous step, it would provoke an attack.

***

Unbeknown to them, however, the Saxons had departed. The recent action had calmed the young chieftain a little and rekindled his confidence in his own capability as a leader, for he had begun to think his standing among the men was waning.

When the Gewisse had been utterly defeated and routed by the Dumnonians, Aldred had taken the disaster badly. Thinking, too, of the other tragedies that had befallen the clan since the beginning of the invasion, he had imagined the men held him solely responsible for their ill fortune. His had been the decision to continue with the invasion, even when the clan's oldest and wisest member had been killed in the first battle by the river. That had been a bad omen and Aldred had chosen not to heed the sign; as a result, Rhinehold had been killed. The man's death had been due entirely to the decision he had made. When Turnstan had gone off into the woods, using himself as a decoy, Aldred had again felt immense guilt; he did not want to be responsible for any more of his clansmen's deaths.

Caradoc's arrival had forced Aldred to face the responsibilities of leadership. For this time, his clan had to fight alone, without the help of others. The last three warriors had been looking to him to get them out of the situation and he had done so with honour. Now he reflected on other incidents, like the time they had broken out of the enclosing Dumnonian trap to flee the lost battle on the moors. On that occasion, they had to run to get away, but when they did have to fight, they'd done so with courage and determination.

Aldred knew now he had changed for the worse when Turnstan had been injured. When Sighelme suggested the path should be cleared of the other dead Dumnonian and pony, Aldred had taken foolish offence; and because of that, the clan had nearly been caught and massacred.

Suddenly, the darkness of night made him feel safer than he had ever felt before and he longed to talk to his cousin Sighelme to apologise for his foolishness, even though as chieftain, he had no need to make excuses for his decisions and Sighelme certainly wouldn't expect him to.

Aldred fell into jogging beside Sighelme, and he whispered, "You were right and I was wrong when I refused to listen to you and drag the dead pony off the pathway. My foolishness and stubbornness have allowed the enemy to track us down and cost Turnstan his life."

"It was not your fault Turnstan died, Aldred," replied Sighelme. "He would not have lasted long with that wound of his."

"No, Sighelme, please," insisted Aldred. "It was my decision that brought about his death. If I had listened to you, Turnstan might still have survived. I am not talking to you in search of pity; I have done you a wrong and am admitting it.

"As chieftain of what remains of this clan, I am not required to apologise for my wrong decisions. Only through loyalty and faith to my clan do I say to you, Sighelme, you were right, I was wrong."

So forceful were his words that he completely won over Sighelme, who still wanted to try and console him in some way, though he said nothing, sensing Aldred might yet be just as volatile as before. He glanced back to where Aldred was now splashing through the water alone. Arrogant he might be, but of his nobility, there was no doubt.

***

The Dumnonians had made little headway in the dark. Hearing groans from further upstream where the ambush had taken place, they suspected a trap, for they thought a large number of Saxons lay in wait for them.

When most of the night had passed without a sign of the enemy, Caradoc began to get impatient. The moaning of the injured man was crushing their resolve and when he set off towards him with two warriors, it was more through irritation than out of pity.

Finding the crude wooden implement which had caused the man's grievous wound and a dead pony with its throat cut, Caradoc was intrigued. Surveying the area, his fears of a renewed attack diminished.

Up on the bank, one of the warriors discovered footprints and called Caradoc over. He looked down at them and sighed. A small number of Saxons had made them look completely foolish by creating a very elaborate and cunning trick and he couldn't help feeling a grudging respect for his enemy.

CHAPTER FIFTEEN

The Saxons continued along the stream, which was getting deeper now. Too afraid to stop and cook the horseflesh, instead they washed it clean of blood and ate it raw. They didn't even stop to do that, for it was now fear feeding them—fear that strengthened their legs. When the water became too deep and the stream had become a small river, the four men took to the bank.

Aldred found himself fighting a phobia that was beginning to swell up inside him and threatened to engulf him. It was as if thousands of eyes were staring at him from out of the gloom. The river sounded as though it was whispering and the young chieftain began to wish he could hear the barking of the hounds again.

"Master Aldred," whispered Wilfred timidly. It was the first time the youth had ever addressed him and all at once, Aldred lost his fear of the night as calmness settled over him. He felt flattered Wilfred had approached him, for he was usually very timid and had been terrified of Leofstan.

"What is it, Wilfred?" he asked, with paternal indulgence. He was unaware Wilfred had come to him because he had noticed his chieftain's fear and wished to help him. Had Aldred realised this, he'd have felt insulted.

"How long do you think we shall remain in the forest?" asked Wilfred. "When shall we reach the hills?"

"I really do not know, Wilfred, but I promise that you will return home safely. With our own courage and determination and the gods' guidance, we shall pull through this ordeal.

"You must be bold, Wilfred. Let Woden see into your innermost self, let him feel your brave spirit. Then he will say, 'This brave soul is worthy of my attention'. If you do this, then Woden will be able to combine all our determination and use it against the Celts."

Smiling, Wilfred made formal and polite thanks for Aldred's words of encouragement and dropped back a few paces. He felt Aldred had spoken to him as though he were a child, whereas Wilfred felt himself to be well aware of their dilemma and had conducted himself quite adequately so far in the campaign and surely with enough honour to be regarded as a warrior.

But as far as Aldred was concerned, Wilfred was still a peasant of low intellect, deserving only a childish explanation to keep up morale.

Sighelme, noticing how Aldred had handled Wilfred, wanted to go over to talk to the youth, but he knew Aldred would jump to the conclusion he was being plotted against and he certainly wanted to avoid a return to the former tension. Aldred was beginning to win his own mental battle. Although Wilfred had been demoralized by what he thought was contempt, he little knew that in fact, he had raised the young chieftain's morale by appearing to look to him, rather than Sighelme for encouragement. There were lessons in diplomacy for both to learn.

Morning crept upon them unawares, for a mist hovered above the ground, hiding the dead ferns and tree roots. Even the surface of the river was becoming hard to see through the mist.

In telling them all to take care, Aldred managed to break the gloomy silence which had hung over them for some time. They became aware of the birdsong all around them and the tranquility gave each warrior a pleasant feeling; for a while, their predicament was forgotten. They had lived to see another morning.

The dampness soon caused Wilfred to start coughing and he looked up into Sighelme's sad eyes. He knew why no one ever mentioned consumption in front of him.

Cuthbert began to reflect on death. His morbid curiosity was always dwelling on the subject and how he would face it. He almost wished they could end their ordeal here, while they were at peace with the morning.

Aldred's hopes of a safe return home were rising with the sun, as yet unseen on the eastern horizon.

Suddenly, the forest ended. The river twisted to the north, forming a boundary between the trees on the west bank and the gently rising moors on the east. The dishevelled band stopped and contemplated the abrupt change in terrain. At first, they were greatly relieved; but then they realised the open ground would give them no cover. Although the morning mist lingered over the slopes, it was broken in parts and they caught glimpses of the green and inviting turf.

"We must not let the direct route tempt us," said Aldred.

"Aye," agreed Cuthbert, "more danger lies in wait for us along that path than any other we might choose to follow."

Their next move needed careful consideration and they all made themselves as comfortable as they could, squatting on the damp ground.

"Our main concern," said Aldred, "is that we are leaving a dangerously easy trail for our hunters to follow. Their hounds will have no trouble in leading them here, so we shall have to try to put them off the scent. It means taking to the water again and swimming, despite the cold. Obviously, we cannot swim the river for any great length of time. Our progress would be much too slow and they'd soon catch up with us.

"I suggest we swim across to the opposite bank and go a little way up the slope to make them believe we have chosen the direct route. Instead, we shall travel in an arc and come back down to the river further along, then swim back to this side at intervals.

"This might confuse them for a while and buy us enough time to increase our lead—if we don't meet any other roving bands, of course."

Aldred looked around at the three warriors. Sighelme had been staring into the river nodding his approval all the time, and Wilfred looked him in the eyes and nodded, saying, "Yes, Master Aldred." Cuthbert said nothing, but just stood, resigned to getting on with the task at hand.

Rising to his feet, Aldred said, "Very well. We move now, while the mist still offers us cover out on the slopes."

As they waded into the river, the cold water was an abrupt shock to their wretched bodies. They moved as fast as possible, but had no need to swim as the water was only chest height. Emerging on the opposite bank, the morning wind against their wet clothes chilled them through to the bone.

Wilfred and Cuthbert took off their breeches, feeling the cold wind would dry wet skin more quickly than wet clothing.

"We should have taken our clothes off and held them above our heads while we were crossing this cursed river," said Sighelme. Swearing at their lack of foresight, all they wanted was to curl up in some crude shelter and let the cold take them but, gritting their teeth, they began to jump up and down in place in order to try and warm themselves a little.

Having restored their circulation, they soon began to regain their determination to continue with their journey.

Up into the moor they ran for a short time, veering northward along the scarp until Aldred decided they had ascended far enough. It was here he had another idea. He told the others to urinate, one next to each other, from here to the summit. This caused much laughter and slight embarrassment amongst the men, but they did it nonetheless.

When they descended to the river again, Sighelme suggested they remove their clothing. They were no longer wearing breeches—Wilfred and Cuthbert had cast theirs aside where the party had first crossed the river, believing their Celtic pursuers would be tempted into the moors by such a find. Now each man stripped off his filthy tunic and put it into the concave dip of his shield, along with his spatha and scarmasax. All spears were thrown across onto the opposite bank before the second crossing was begun. Everyone entered the water naked, apart from shoes and leg-bindings.

Reaching the other side, the forest provided a screen against the wind, making the morning chill a little more bearable, and they all began to exercise their limbs again.

"The day will soon begin to warm us up," said Cuthbert.

"Yes, but until then, we must keep on the move," said Aldred anxiously.

Wilfred rested his spear on his shoulders and hung his garments from them to dry. The rest copied his idea and soon, the four naked men began to follow the river, looking more like a bunch of old washing women than warriors.

***

Although Caradoc was convinced the Saxons had departed, he decided it would be profitable to wait until the morning before continuing with the hunt.

Gryffith was in bad spirits that morning. His head ached from the wine he had drunk and now he was beginning to brood over the lost chance of catching the Saxons. He glared at Caradoc, sitting alone at the edge of the stream, keeping his own counsel, and burst out, "In the name of God, how much longer must we wait here?"

The Gwentman remained silent for a while before answering, knowing this would aggravate the young man.

Eventually, he said, "It will soon be light enough to see our enemies' footprints. Then we shall know exactly how many we are hunting."

"What does it matter about their exact number? All we need to worry about is catching them. Anyway, you said there weren't many of them."

Caradoc rose to his feet looking grim. Gryffith reminded him of a bug, a niggling, irritating parasite, and he longed to tell him so. Instead, he decided to argue and try to humiliate him. The youngster could never resist an argument and often left himself wide open for Caradoc's verbal backlash.

Very calmly, the older man began, "It matters to me. I want to know as much about them as possible. Just because they're few in number, I certainly do not intend to underestimate them.

"As for you, Gryffith—you are a leader of sufficient men to search for Saxons in whatever way you think best. I shall stick with my own methods."

Unperturbed, Gryffith argued, "We each have an army to consider. Our men are now dispersed throughout the wood in small groups, hunting down all those little bands of Saxons who managed to escape. Suppose they manage to reorganise and we run into them with the numbers we have here? We'll have no chance—they'll massacre us, all because we foolishly decided to hunt down a small band of Saxons."

Caradoc proceeded in slow, methodical sentences to demolish his argument, "Who told you to leave and disperse your forces throughout the forest? The chance of a large group of Saxons regrouping without being observed by our patrols is negligible. If it did happen, we would hear the horns blowing all over the forest.

"Finally, the risk of dying by meeting a large Saxon force is less than that of being slain by a small one." With that, Caradoc was gone, while the Dumnonian was still searching for a reply.

Though speechless with fury, Gryffith's sense of decorum prevented him from creating a scene outright and he reluctantly conceded for the time being. Inwardly, however, he swore revenge. His young pride had been hurt by a man he considered beneath him and his immaturity could not accept such a rebuke.

He watched Caradoc with hate-filled eyes while the Gwentman called his warriors from their uncomfortable slumber, putting them to the task of searching out the positions from which the individual Saxon warriors had started their ambush.

CHAPTER SIXTEEN

By midmorning, Caradoc, Gryffith and their men had reached the edge of the forest, where they had a clear view of the moor, unlike Aldred's band earlier. They could see where the desperate little band of Saxons had entered the water and Gryffith said, with grudging admiration, "Those four have tricked and evaded us right across this forest."

"Yes," agreed Caradoc with a sigh. About to mention the bravery of the fifth Saxon who had died fighting the hounds after leading them astray, he checked himself, realizing Gryffith might assume he was being ridiculed, which would cause another argument. He'd remained solemn ever since their last clash.

Caradoc was first to cross the river and had been sitting on his pony contemplating Cuthbert's and Wilfred's breeches for some time before Gryffith decided to follow. The youth had wanted him to notice he had chosen to come across in his own time, rather than follow at the older man's heels, and for a while, he was gratified when Caradoc's men innocently decided to wait with him. This soon turned to frustration, however, when he saw Caradoc had not even bothered to turn his head and call to them, being far too interested in the abandoned garments and tracks left behind by the Saxons.

Gryffith was curious, too, in spite of himself, and rode up alongside Caradoc. He looked down at the discarded garments. "After showing such skill in their bid to escape, they have finally panicked and fled onto the open moorlands. They'll not get far on foot now, especially in daylight."

But Caradoc was lost in his own thoughts. He'd soon realized why the Saxons had discarded their breeches, and seen through the ploy.

"Well, what do you make of it?" asked Gryffith.

Looking up to the summit, Caradoc replied, "I don't think they have taken to the moors—they're just trying to trick us into believing they have." He turned to his men and said, "Bring the hounds!" Dismounting, he grasped the Saxon clothing and rubbed each animal's muzzle into it, making sure the beasts had the scent. The trail was soon picked up and within seconds, the hounds were pulling impatiently at their leashes.

Off they all went, and as the hounds began to move parallel to the scarp, Caradoc knew the trail would eventually lead back to the river.

But suddenly, the hounds turned towards the summit, then stopped to sniff more eagerly at certain areas of ground and urinate upon it. Investigating, he discovered they were reacting to human urine.

"The bastards have pissed up the slope to distract the hounds," he grinned.

"Very crafty," agreed Gryffith.

"They intend to follow the river until it reaches the coast. This river twists and turns to the northeast—we could cut across the moors and reach its mouth long before they do."

"Why not continue to pursue them along the river?" argued Gryffith.

"Because if they do realize we are on their trail again, they'll be forced to run deeper into the forest, away from the river. They might even get away and then come upon the river at another point."

Tired of taking Caradoc's advice, Gryffith chose to follow the river with his band of warriors, while the Gwentman went his own way.

Caradoc made no attempt to dissuade him, for he'd found the arrogant youngster's company taxing. Before leaving Gryffith, Caradoc offered the hounds, stressing that he had no need of them himself. Gryffith accepted the offer, though without thanks.

***

Further downstream, Aldred and his men trudged wearily onwards. They were dry now, for the morning sun had considerable warmth—though not enough to dry their wet clothes, so they remained naked. None of them had any experience with such extreme physical endurance and all were feeling the strain. Muscles tightened throughout their bodies, especially in the legs and back.

Wilfred's calves were pulling so tightly, he knew he'd soon be unable to continue, but he struggled inwardly to force himself to keep up with the rest of the group.

Despite their fatigue, Aldred, Sighelme and Cuthbert all felt more able to accept the situation whilst continuously moving; whenever they stopped, the same terrible flutterings of fear flowered in the pit of their stomachs.

Sighelme, by far the fittest, ran a little way ahead to observe the lie of the land and so was the first to see the Dumnonians coming up on the other side of the river. At once, he dropped flat on his stomach, ignoring the cold chill of the wet grass against his naked skin. His only concern was that Aldred would have seen his movements, but he need not have worried, for Aldred had seen and understood and made sure that Wilfred and Cuthbert flattened themselves along with him. Such a command was a blessed relief to Wilfred, who needed so desperately to rest, he cared not for the reasons.

They only just managed to hide in time before about fifty Dumnonians came around the bend—

fifteen on horseback and the rest on foot.

The all-too-familiar flutterings of fear blossomed once more within the four men watching from the limited security of their hiding places. Men on foot were carrying poles from which dangled several Saxon heads, such was their pride in their recent victories.

Soon the enemy force disappeared from view behind a screen of trees and Sighelme came running back to Aldred. "That lot are almost certain to meet the ones who are still tracking us down," he said anxiously.

"They might assume our heads are among those on the poles," said Aldred hopefully.

Rather cautiously and politely for fear of angering him, Cuthbert pointed out that was rather unlikely; but Aldred was too tired to react and besides, Cuthbert was one of the few people with whom he found it impossible to get angry.

Wearily, he agreed and added, "That was more what I hope than what I believe. We have to keep moving; the need for haste is even greater now."

As they were preparing to move on, it was discovered Wilfred was in such pain, he could no longer continue the journey without help. Completely exhausted, his body throbbed all over from the strain of ceaseless running. He was now in agony, for stopping had made him much worse. The others regarded him sympathetically, for their legs, too, were suffering, though not so badly.

"We'll have to take turns carrying him," said Aldred, and all agreed immediately, though they realized this would slow down their own progress and jeopardize their chances of escape. But how could they leave one of their own clan members to die, when there was a glimmer of hope they might just make it back home together? They were all committed to one another's well-being.

When they'd put on their damp clothes—for they could not carry those as well as Wilfred—Aldred cut down a branch, strong enough to take the lad's weight. He and Sighelme clasped the ends firmly, while Cuthbert helped Wilfred to sit upon the branch between them.

They were going to abandon the wooden stakes they had made, but Aldred was reluctant to do this. Wilfred managed to awkwardly hold his own spear, plus two of the stakes in one hand, while holding onto Sighelme with the other. Cuthbert, leading the way, carried the rest of the stakes.

Their progress, though slower, was nonetheless noticeable and they were heartened. Neither Aldred nor Sighelme showed any outward sign of weakening, for the cousins had always harboured a jealous rivalry towards one another over physical endurance; even under these circumstances, the old competitiveness was still there. Aldred, being a much more openly aggressive character, had often allowed his jealous resentment to show, so people were led to believe that he alone was the competitor. Sighelme, a much calmer person, was able to contain his feelings, but his own desire to outdo Aldred was just as strong, as Aldred well knew.

Both men were aware that in matters of endurance, Sighelme usually fared better, but Aldred had a raw stubbornness, which sometimes brought him through. This competitiveness might well prove to be an asset with this added burden which had descended upon them.

Cuthbert, ahead, kept his eyes and ears alert for signs of the enemy and towards afternoon, he caught sight of a reddish tinge in the water.

"Aldred," he called, "there's blood in the river!"

Aldred and Sighelme stopped and carefully put Wilfred down with his back against an ash tree.

"Shall I go ahead and explore?" asked Sighelme.

"Yes, I'll come with you," replied Aldred.

They did not have to go far before the water was red from the bank and neither was surprised to see the butchered, headless corpses of twelve Saxons lying scattered about. As the two men approached the scene, a number of crows and a few gulls flew up into the air, squawking angrily and a frightened stoat fled to the moor.

"The wolves will soon be here to feast," observed Sighelme bitterly.

"They're probably getting fat on all the Gewisse lying around the forest," agreed Aldred.

When they'd satisfied themselves there were no weapons or anything else useful among the dead, Sighelme tentatively suggested returning to Cuthbert and Wilfred.

"You go back for Cuthbert and Wilfred," said Aldred. His voice held a note of excitement. "I have an idea that may throw our pursuers completely off our scent."

Sighelme hurried off and found Cuthbert trying to lift Wilfred on his own.

"What are you doing?" he asked.

"I've seen a large group of horsemen coming this way," explained Cuthbert. "They'll be here very soon."

"We must be quick then," agreed Sighelme.

Wilfred was able to stand by himself and even walk a little, but he'd have been too slow. He was given the spears to hold while Sighelme and Cuthbert continued to carry him seated on the branch.

Aldred was removing the breeches from a Saxon corpse when they arrived and Sighelme told him what Cuthbert had seen.

"Quickly, then. Each of you must take a pair of breeches off a man, then urinate over that particular corpse. The hounds know our smell and we may be able to trick them into thinking our bodies are among these dead men. These Dumnonians who had been hunting us must know by now we're not wearing breeches and four bare-legged bodies may be all that is needed to convince them we are dead, especially if they ran into the Dumnonians who passed us earlier this morning. They would report no sighting of us," said Aldred.

"What if they are not fooled by our disguise?" asked Cuthbert, putting Aldred's plan into action.

"Then there is no hope for us."

"We'd have to make a last stand here," added Sighelme.

Finally, they scattered the crude stakes about, hoping with this further evidence to convince the Dumnonians that they were dead.

That done, they entered the river, Sighelme carrying Wilfred on his back. All four managed to hide beneath the exposed roots of an elm tree where the bank had been eroded away, and here they waited to observe their enemy hunters.

***

In a very short time, Gryffith came upon the headless Saxon corpses and led his party across the forested side of the bank. Earlier, he had been delighted to meet with the large force of Dumnonians, for among them were a contingent of his own men led by a warrior called Ythel.

When Ythel told him of his attack on a group of Saxons, the young chieftain had asked if there were four men among them without breeches. No one could be certain, so Gryffith had decided to investigate for himself, taking his own warriors, plus some of Ythel's horsemen.

He noticed the wooden stakes at once, and when the hounds began to tear at some of the dead warriors, Gryffith observed the bodies had no breeches.

"Yes, they are here," he said. "It is a pity—I'd have liked to have caught up with them myself. Caradoc will be disappointed."

"Caradoc, my lord?" echoed Ythel, somewhat confused. He'd not known Gryffith and Caradoc had been searching for the fugitive Saxons together.

"Yes, he has taken his men across the moors to where the river flows into the sea. He will be disappointed to hear of the death of these particular Saxons." The young chieftain sat silent for a moment, then burst out, "I want Caradoc dead, Ythel. If I am to succeed and rule over this land, he must go. There can be no room for both of us. If we cut across the moor now, we shall be able to slay him and his men. We'll have to take the footmen with us, too."

"Shall we ride back for them now, my lord?" asked Ythel obediently.

"Yes," replied Gryffith.

***

Aldred and his men watched as the enemy warriors rode off the way they had come. Sighelme alone understood Gaelic and although he could only hear pieces of the conversation, he was able to learn the Dumnonians had been fooled by Aldred's idea and they aimed to kill Caradoc. But he did not catch the bit about Caradoc lying in wait for them at the mouth of the river. Aldred was surprised to hear of their intentions, for he did not know Caradoc had a rival. Unaware there were two chieftains, the Saxons suspected it was a plot among Caradoc's own men; and they remained ignorant of the fact Caradoc was hunting them.

Once the Saxons were sure Gryffith and his force were well away, they emerged from their hiding place. At Aldred's suggestion, they put on the clothes of some of the dead and even took extra items to keep themselves warm at night. Dry, the clothes certainly were; but they were also stained with the blood of the dead.

Now that they were no longer being pursued, they thought it safe to try to sleep until nightfall—a welcome idea to them all, having been on the move continuously since vespers the day before.

Away from the edge of the river, they found an ideal place to sleep where they could not be spotted by anyone out on the moor. Beneath a huge sycamore tree, there was an abundance of foliage offering inviting cover, into which they crawled gratefully.

Cuthbert took the first watch.

CHAPTER SEVENTEEN

At about the same time Aldred and his men were settling themselves down to rest, Caradoc and his riders arrived at the river's mouth where it met the sea. Sitting motionless on his horse, he stared dreamily northwards across the water in the direction of Gwent, the kingdom from which he had been banished.

Lost in this thoughts of remembering his younger days, he was jolted out of it by one of his men asking if he could lead a patrol up the river, in search of the four Saxons.

"No," said Caradoc, "we shall rest here until nightfall. I think the Saxons could well shake Gryffith and his men off their trail. Although they'd never actually abandon the river as a guide, Gryffith could easily be tricked into thinking they would. My guess is our shrewd enemies rest by day and follow the river by night—in which case, they'll have to pass this spot and we shall be waiting for them."

The young Dumnonian listened intently, nodding when he'd finished, but still looking confused.

Recognizing this, Caradoc said kindly, "You seem troubled. May I help?"

The youth hesitated for a moment before answering his chieftain. "Well, my Lord, I was wondering why you had sent two of our men back into the forest for reinforcements when we are only hunting four of the Saxon fugitives."

"The Saxon army that invaded this land is no longer a threat," began Caradoc. "What we do now in hunting them is…" Here he hesitated, as though searching for the right words, "Nothing more than barbaric, unchristian and wicked sport.

"Our enemy is now Gryffith. He leaves us no choice. He is headstrong and talks to people however he likes, provoking verbal reprisals he cannot swallow. I'm afraid I have wounded his foolish pride, and now, he means to have his revenge on me. None of my followers know where I am, except for you people here, less than twenty of us. Gryffith knows this, and being so near the forest, he could start to recruit his own men for the task of killing us all here. If he does, he's going to be very surprised when he sees our numbers greatly reinforced."

"Will you kill him?" asked the youth.

"No, not unless I have to and I don't suppose that's very likely. Gryffith hasn't the courage for an honourable fight." Caradoc looked back across the moors, the way he and his warriors had come. "I feel sure Gryffith will try to betray and kill us, but I have no wish to fight his forces.

"Without the fragile alliance that exists between Gryffith and myself against the Saxons—their tribesmen would already have taken another chunk out of Celtic lands. These pagan races would gradually pursue their ruthless ambitions until every last Celt is driven into the sea.

"For the time being, this has been avoided, but with the sweeping aside of the Saxons, the old danger of feudalism is beginning to raise it's ugly head once more.

"However, this one small defeat of the pagans will not deter them from trying again. I know they have only launched a half-hearted invasion. Next time, it will almost certainly be much better organized, with King Ceawlin at the head of a larger army.

"If Dumnonia is to stand any chance of halting them, her chieftains must be in resolute alliance— determined and steadfast in the face of such a fierce enemy."

"But you doubt such chieftains as Gryffith?" The younger man had been listening intently.

Caradoc nodded his affirmation. "Yet he does command noble men and to make an enemy of such a leader, no matter how lacking in courage, would only foster resentment among the good, faithful men who follow him."

"What will you do?" asked the youth.

"I hope to counter the spread of corruption Gryffith might cause with a simple show of force. From now on, I must try to persuade other chieftains from the west to come and help maintain the important border defenses. With more noblemen allied to the cause, Gryffith would be very unwise to make an enemy of me."

Dismounting, Caradoc handed the reins to one of his men, then found a place apart from the others and squatted on his haunches to look down upon the sea as its waves broke on the scattered boulders and rolled over the golden sands. It was likely to be quite a long wait: if the Saxons had managed to lose Gryffith, they would surely rest for the remainder of the day, and so, would not pass the Dumnonian ambush until night. His mind moved on, wondering which direction Gryffith would come from if he were to attack. Certainly not from along the river, as the young chieftain would know Caradoc would be watching that route for the Saxons. No, if Gryffith should try to betray him, the attack would come from behind, the way Caradoc himself had come.

Unnerved by the thought, he shook himself out of his reverie to send two men back a little way along the path he and his warriors had covered, bidding them find suitable cover and keep watch for any movement.

Caradoc's men were beginning to grow restless over their chieftain's devotion to the hunting of four Saxons when there were plenty more lost in the forest. The futility of it made them feel more vulnerable to Gryffith's suspected treachery, though their loyalty and respect stopped them from questioning Caradoc's decision. He had always adopted the right strategy in the past; they all felt bound to silence, accepting their numbers would increase soon enough and vanquish the existing problems.

***

Aldred's afternoon passed without incident and all four men were able to get enough sleep for the journey ahead. The fact their trackers had been fooled and no longer searched for them was a weight off their minds. Wilfred could at least walk unaided now, albeit slowly and in considerable discomfort.

Although it was a long time until nightfall, they were all keen to get on their way—not that they thought it the safest course to follow, rather that none of them liked staying in one spot. The uncertainty of their predicament made them edgy, and only on the move was this partially abated.

They set off very slowly, at little more than a dawdle, for Wilfred's efforts at walking, though determined, were very slow. To keep themselves hidden from any prying eyes out on the moors, they traveled just inside the forest, keeping the river in earshot.

All the time, hunger raised its insistent demands on them. Every shrub they passed was investigated, to see if its fruits were those they knew to be edible. When it was something they did not recognise, they were frustrated, knowing they might be leaving something nourishing in case it was poisonous.

Hazelnuts they knew, and found aplenty, despite the squirrels' and birds' partiality for them. If the nuts were green, they ate them immediately, storing the brown ones.

Cuthbert sighed. "A woman would have known what to pick. It makes one realize how valuable a women's chores are in the maintenance of our way of life. I recall, somewhat ruefully, how often we scorn and mock nagging woman who complain about their tasks."

The others smiled in agreement. "But don't ever let them know you said such a thing," laughed Sighelme.

"Yes," agreed Aldred. "You would never hear the end of it."

Sighelme and Wilfred collected an edible fungus, canterelle, the colour of egg yolk and with a sweet, fruity smell. This fungus was rarely attacked by insects and could not be confused with any dangerous species. They found wild turnip, which they would boil in water, crush and squeeze out the juice, then eat the mashed remains. Mixed in with the turnip would be a small plant with white flowers containing five petals on a fragile stem, its leaves shaped like the shamrock.

"Do you think we'll reach the river's mouth by nightfall, Aldred?" asked Cuthbert hopefully. The young man's enthusiasm heartened Aldred. It was good to see his spirits high, despite their predicament.

"I certainly hope and pray to Woden that we may," he replied.

Wilfred then spoke up, "Please forgive me for being the cause of your slower pace, Masters."

"Cuthbert and I are no longer your masters, Wilfred," said Sighelme.

"Yes, indeed," agreed Aldred, "you are now one of my warriors: a Gewisse warrior. I have seen with my own eyes your courage and determination in battle. For you, Wilfred, born of the slave class, there can be no higher honor to bestow upon you than that of a freeman like the rest of us. You are most certainly our equal in every way.

"My father, though not high enough to command the rights of Brookland, was able to acquire the deeds that go with the laws from a high lord, who did command such power, the only Gewisse Saxon, in fact, to whom Ceawlin has granted such authority. These deeds of your freedom were to be presented to you after what we all expected to be a victorious campaign against Dumnonia and you were to have a substantial share of the lands we won, with a number of hides to start you off. Now, in our defeat, even when we do get back home, I am sure King Ceawlin will be punishing all the Gewisse with harsh land retributions.

"But when my father was killed, these deeds became my responsibility. I had intended to save the presentation until we made it back home—but not anymore, for I am sure our return will mark the beginning of new problems. Therefore, I think now is an appropriate time to give you these deeds..." He paused reflectively, then added, "This makes me very happy." With these words, he took a small Rune stone from his woollen jersey and held it out to Wilfred, adding, "I am sorry I do not understand the markings, but I'm assured it is genuine. It is sufficient proof for any nobleman in the West Saxon Lands who may ask for you to show evidence of your freedom."

Lost for words, Wilfred felt happiness bubbling up inside him as he realized how wrong he'd been about Aldred, and tears of emotion sprang to his eyes. He'd been convinced his new chieftain would barely even acknowledge his existence, yet here he was, presenting him with his freedom—with the most heart-lifting of commendations.

Even Sighelme and Cuthbert were surprised by Aldred's presentation and Cuthbert said majestically, "Indeed, Lord Aldred," knowing that Aldred alone was sufficient to address his chieftain in the lax custom of the small, close-knit communities of the dying Gewisse tribes. "If I live to be old, I am sure no chieftain will ever make such a happy and joyous decision as this."

Sighelme agreed in like terms and Aldred was stunned by such extreme respect.

"Thank you, my Lord," said Wilfred, as he took the small stone rune—his sacred treasure. Although none could understand the markings, the neatly scrawled lines brought him untold joy and for a few moments, they were all merry beneath the trees of hostile Dumnonia on that beautiful September day.

But soon, more urgent matters began to nag at them. As cordially as possible, Aldred pressed them now to continue with their journey.

They strolled along at Wilfred's pace, which allowed them time to observe everything in the forest's lush greenness. Despite the feeling their presence was still unwelcome, fear no longer gripped them at this moment and they diverted themselves by trying to determine the names of the trees, to feed and maintain the happiness they had shared in Wilfred's social advancement.

Cuthbert was the main source of entertainment, talking of all the birds and animals that dwelt within the forest, bringing a different view of the area from the more evil one they'd had up to now. They all realised, of course, there was no difference between Dumnonian and West Saxon woodland—the animals, birds and plants were just the same. For a short time, the dangers of the forest were lost from their minds.

All at once, Aldred told everyone to stop and keep quiet. They strained their ears to listen, but at first, all they could hear were the familiar sounds of the forest: the rustling leaves, the birds and the now fast-flowing river, hidden from their sight by a screen of trees and bushes. But then, in the distance, they heard the sound of voices—Celtic voices.

"There's quite a commotion going on," said Sighelme.

"Yes," agreed Aldred, "and right in our path, too."

"Perhaps there's a track up ahead that leads to the river," suggested Cuthbert.

"There might even be a ferry, too—that would explain why there's so much noise," said Sighelme.

"There's only one way to find out." Aldred crouched down and took the lead, off towards the enemy sound. The others followed, equally cautiously, and as they got nearer, they all began to feel the familiar pangs of fear.

Telling the others to wait, Aldred crawled ahead on his own. He could feel his heart pumping throughout his body, as though wishing to distribute the burden evenly, but a heavy lump in his chest remained undiminished. Reaching an old oak tree, he hid behind it and cautiously peeped around the trunk.

Before him on the pathway of dried mud, a group of about twenty Dumnonians were standing by the river next to a small, wooden jetty. A little distance away was a small, crude hut, fashioned from branches and covered with animal hides. Aldred was surprised to see how wide the river was here. A raft, punted by two ferrymen, was approaching the waiting warriors. On the opposite bank was a larger contingent, who had presumably already been transported across. There were about thirty footmen led by three mounted warriors.

The horsemen were facing the south, the direction from which Aldred and his men had come, and he wondered whether these Dumnonians were going to join the force that had recently been pursuing his group.

He watched with mounting interest as the raft docked at the jetty, where the rest of the enemy clambered aboard in a noisy, disorderly manner. Within seconds, the craft was casting off again.

Returning to his companions, he told them of his find. They would now rest until dawn, he said, and when night fell, they'd steal the raft and head down the river towards the sea. Soon, they heard the ferrymen return and Aldred checked to ensure that they were alone. They were.

With the bright new prospect of travelling on the raft instead of their weary legs, the four fugitives settled down to wait. Nobody spoke because of the ferrymen being close at hand. Wilfred and Sighelme dozed, while Cuthbert sat lost in his thoughts. Aldred kept watch—alone, silent and aloof.

At last, night came. No one else had come along requiring the services of the ferry and the four men thought it highly unlikely anyone would before morning.

From the hut where the two boatmen were sheltering came the flicker of a fire and Gaelic chatter.

"These men are certainly not expecting danger, even though they know there are many of us fugitive Saxons at large," whispered Cuthbert.

"It would seem so," agreed Aldred. "Let's move now."

As quietly as possible, they began to sneak up towards the clearing with swords drawn, for it was their intention to slay the ferrymen before taking the raft.

They were about to emerge onto the pathway, when Cuthbert again whispered. "Stop!" They instantly froze and looked at him enquiringly.

"There are two coracles here at my feet," he hissed. "They will suit our needs better."

"Coracles?" echoed Aldred, puzzled.

"Yes, come and look."

They all crept over to him, looked down and saw two little round boats, consisting of a fragile wooden frame covered with deer hide. Aldred recognised them from his childhood. When he was an infant, many of the Dumnonian slaves had used such craft on the river. They were so light, a man could carry one on his back. He thought for a moment and then said, "Do you think that these, er..."

"Coracles," put in Cuthbert.

"Yes, thank you," he muttered testily. He hated being corrected, although his morale was much better than it had been on previous nights.

Cuthbert smiled apprehensively.

"These coracles will be able to hold two of us," said Aldred, changing what was to be a question into a statement, "and so the ferrymen's lives must be spared. It's quite likely more Dumnonians will be using the crossing when daylight comes—if they see the ferrymen dead and the raft stolen, they will surely realize we'll be following the river back to the coast.

'If, on the other hand, we take the coracles, the ferrymen could continue to use the raft without discovering their small boats have been stolen."

With as little noise as possible, they picked up the coracles, along with oars, which were lying beside them, and walked cautiously along the path onto the wooden jetty. Lowering the coracles into the black, murky water, they paused for a moment, checking to ensure the ferrymen had not heard them. Sighelme and Wilfred climbed in and clung to the sides as the vessel swayed dangerously. Once it had stabilized, Sighelme began to row out into the darkness. Every now and then, Wilfred put his arm into the water, trying to use it as a crude oar. Aldred and Cuthbert followed in the other coracle.

The moon was full, but as it was a cloudy night, the two parties frequently lost visual contact with each other. They allowed the current to take them, knowing it would bring them to their destination. Only when they neared the banks did they put any real effort into paddling. Most of the time, they were preoccupied with keeping their weight evenly distributed in the flimsy craft.

Although the young men came from a seafaring race—and not many generations back, either, for still they referred to the unseen Rhinelands as 'home'— they were quite ignorant of the coracle's efficiency, despite the fact the slaves in their own colonized territories had been known to use them.

The claustrophobia of the night before no longer plagued them now, maybe because there was no one pursuing them as far as they could tell; and now that the river was wider and deeper, they felt more secure. They feared only the dawn, when daylight would allow enemy eyes to see them. No one spoke. There was nothing to say, just another night to travel through and a day to spend in hiding.

CHAPTER EIGHTEEN

Gryffith had been scheming to kill Caradoc in order to gain complete control of those territories of eastern Dumnonia invaded by the Saxons.

It was night and he had stopped his force a little way inland from where Caradoc and his followers were camped. The young chieftain knew Caradoc would have his men watching the horizon, looking for him.

Gryffith was beginning to think that maybe he had taken on an opponent who was more than a match for his devious ways. Caradoc certainly seemed to have read his mind too well. He had hoped to kill Caradoc and his small band of men during the day, but as time went by and he realized he could not approach unobserved, he held back. But he could not back down from his plan because his men would question his ability to lead, even though they had no stomach for the task at hand. They had accepted his reason for postponing the attack until the early morning as feasible. Obviously, an attack during the night was not wise because it would be too difficult to keep the force together. Also, a few of Caradoc's men would probably escape into the darkness and get word to their fellows who were still searching the forest for the fugitives. If this happened, Gryffith's plan to pass off Caradoc's death as being slain fighting a large band of Saxons would fail.

No, if his plan were to succeed, all Caradoc's companions must die.

Gryffith stood and walked up to the summit. For protection against the cold night wind, he wore a thick deer hide wrapped around him, as did all his men. The young chieftain had forbidden fires for fear of giving away their position. This order was very unpopular, for the wind was vicious on the open moorlands, even in summer. The warriors huddled together, coughing and complaining about the rheumatic pains from which most of them suffered.

Ythel got up, preferring to exercise his limbs, rather than let them stiffen in the night chill. He climbed to the top of the small moor in search of Gryffith, whom he had seen heading in that direction. The ascent was difficult in the dark, clouds having moved across to obliterate the moon and stars.

Cursing as he slipped and slid a few feet down the smooth turf, Ythel wanted to call out to Gryffith, but refrained, not wishing to anger him. Ythel felt Gryffith had become much more erratic and extra cautious since he had last been with his Overlord at the big battle. Since then, he knew Gryffith had hunted alongside Caradoc in pursuit of a fleeing Saxon band in the forest. The young chieftain had come away from the adventure with a marked hatred, a burning jealousy towards Caradoc.

Ythel had never met the Gwentman, only seen him from a distance after the hillside battle, but he'd heard a great deal about him. As far as he was concerned, Caradoc was an impressive man who had done a great service to Dumnonia, standing defiantly against the heathen Saxons when the odds were stacked against him. For Ythel, Caradoc deserved a place among the Dumnonian lords—God would never have granted such victories to the Gwentman otherwise.

Trapped between his religious beliefs and his duty to Gryffith, his Overlord, Ythel knew he would always put his allegiance to Gryffith first, unless he received an unquestionable sign from God. But there was no reason why he should not try to dissuade Gryffith from the attack on Caradoc, even if it would make him unpopular among his men.

As he reached the summit, the moon came out from behind a cloud and he signed irritably. Seeing the dark silhouette of Gryffith staring up at the moon, he made his way over to him.

"My Lord," he said, but the words were carried off into the night by the wind. When he tapped Gryffith on the shoulder, the young chieftain jumped round, startled.

Somewhat relieved, he said, "Oh, it's you, Ythel. You frightened me."

"I am sorry, my Lord."

Gryffith smiled, something he never did to a subordinate unless he was worried about something. "It is difficult to sleep on a night like this," he said, in an unexpectedly friendly tone. It made Ythel uncomfortable, for Gryffith had never spoken to him like this before. He was always official, like his father.

"Er, yes, my Lord, it is," agreed Ythel uncertainly.

"Very well, you can tell the men that they may have a fire. I am sure Caradoc's lookouts will not notice the glow on this side of the moor," said Gryffith, thinking he had anticipated Ythel's reason for coming to see him.

"Thank you, my Lord, the men will be pleased," replied Ythel. For a moment, he stood still, wondering how best to broach the subject of Caradoc. He found Gryffith a most difficult man to talk to. Not only did his social rank make serious conversation awkward for a subordinate, but his arrogance and utter contempt for the lower classes made it almost impossible for any of his men to even approach him.

The chieftain looked at Ythel and frowned cynically.

"There was something else, my Lord," said Ythel tentatively.

The frown disappeared, replaced by a much more encouraging look. Ythel relaxed and continued, "It is about Caradoc, my Lord. I was wondering if it would be wise to wait before striking against him. The Saxons may invade again next spring, and if they do, men like Caradoc may be needed to help thwart them. He has, after all, proved himself in the eyes of the peasantry, as indeed have you, my Lord. But it is the Gwentman who commands their respect." He stopped and waited for a reaction.

"How long have you known I have been pondering on this decision about Caradoc?" asked Gryffith, in a very matter-of-fact tone.

The question took Ythel by surprise and he stuttered before he could force out, "I thought the issue may have been troubling you when you went off on your own." The man's intuition was unnerving.

"Does anybody else suspect I am worried about this?" asked Gryffith.

"I do not think so, my Lord. No one has said anything to me," replied Ythel.

"Then this advice you offer is purely your own—something which you have chosen to do on your own initiative?"

"Yes, my Lord." Ythel was beginning to feel nervous with Gryffith's cool and correct assumptions. The young chieftain's attitude was sinister.

Gryffith, turning to face him, could see the man was frightened. Slowly, he walked around Ythel, assessing him. Although he would not show it, Gryffith was really thankful for Ythel's counsel.

"What you say about Caradoc is true," he said. "However, if I delay from acting soon, then the panic-stricken lords in the west will hear of his brave feats. When they know the land is saved from heathen colonisation, Caradoc will be hailed the length and breadth of the country. He will make many powerful and influential friends and I shall not be able to touch him. Therefore, he must die before he can receive the fruits of praise and victory. When I kill him, he will still be a hero, but one who sacrificed his life fighting against pagan aggressors." Gryffith smiled to himself. Ythel had provided him with the means of continuing with his plan. His dedication was renewed.

Now Gryffith stared at Ythel to see if he had anything else to say, but the warrior remained silent. He had given up all hope of dissuading Gryffith from attacking Caradoc. He remembered the way the chieftain had spoken during the day, when he was trying to rally his followers to the cause of killing the Gwentman.

Gryffith knew Ythel disapproved of his reasons for wanting to kill Caradoc, but he made no mention of it. Ythel was honest and devoted to his duty, qualities which Gryffith despised and mocked for himself, but found useful in his followers.

"When the dawn comes," he said, "we shall ride to Caradoc's position. After the deed is done, we shall spread the word of his death at the hands of the Saxons. Many will suspect me, no doubt, but in time, the Gwentman will be forgotten."

"Let us hope he has not changed his position," added Ythel submissively.

"He will wait for them for most of the morning," replied Gryffith confidently. Once again, silence settled on the two men and Gryffith, his spirits rising, began to pace up and down.

Ythel stood watching him for a few moments, embarrassed, before saying, "I will go back and tell the men that they may light fires, then, my Lord."

"Yes," said Gryffith, still pacing, and as Ythel turned to go, he added sharply, "Tell no one of our conversation."

Thankfully, Ythel sped off down the slope into the darkness, feeling totally confused and ashamed of his efforts to talk with Gryffith. The man made a person feel inferior, even though he was bent on fulfilling his own selfish aims. Yet Ythel knew that although Gryffith was interested only in his own selfish ends, he had to dedicate himself, reluctantly, to serving him.

At the bottom of the scarp, Ythel began walking along the bank of the tiny stream, which eased his troubled mind with its musical trickling sound. He plodded on and soon found himself in the middle of the encampment, surrounded by the miserable, shivering men.

"You may light fires," he said and at once, they erupted into excited chatter. Wood was produced seemingly from nowhere on the bleak moors. Perhaps they'd expected him to win the right to light fires and, in anticipation, had brought wood from the forest. They were happy now and willing to do whatever Gryffith, their lord, wanted of them.

Ythel was soon able to forget Gryffith's lust for power and enjoy the company of the rest of the men.

CHAPTER NINETEEN

Caradoc had spent most of the night in lone contemplation on the last stretch of hills before they gave way to a sandy beach and the sea. Further along the shore to the east, white cliffs were visible. The sound of the waves soothed him and he now felt quite calm about the future. He was sure the four Saxons had evaded Gryffith.

The Gwentman had his men watching along the shoreline and the riverbanks. Hunting down the four fugitives had become an obsession—a passion, which he could not dismiss. If he knew ten other Saxons would certainly be caught in another direction, he would not show any interest in them, for his desire to take these four men was above all else. The very thought of them making it back to their own borders and being able to tell of how they had outwitted a large party of Celtic warriors made him tremble with anger. Anybody hearing such a tale would worship the Saxons as heroes, seeing the adventure only through the biased eyes of the talebearers. They would know nothing of Caradoc and his men, of how steadfast and brave the Dumnonians had been, eventually gaining a victory for themselves through their determination. The heathens would simply see overwhelming Dumnonian numbers defeating their small but gallant invasion force. The few courageous Saxons who managed to escape from the battlefield were then hunted down by thousands of dimwitted Dumnonians.

Caradoc tormented himself, imaging the Saxons in their hamlets gathered around a huge fire while their bards told such a story. The Gwentman had been on the end of such distortion once before. Long ago in Gwent, his own brother had manipulated the facts about some things he had done and it had led to his being disowned by his father and left penniless. The king, too, had heard the tales and banished Caradoc from Gwent forever.

He'd had no choice but to leave. Any man would feel bitter about the false accusations that ruined his character, but he knew there was nothing he could do. Besides, he had no desire to remain in Gwent when he saw how readily people believed his brother. Even his own father swallowed it all, and Caradoc felt ashamed of him, angry he could be so easily duped.

Caradoc lost no time in leaving the country of his birth, crossing the small channel that separated Gwent from Dumnonia, planning to travel further south across the sea to Gaul.

When he arrived on Dumnonian shores, he found a land already troubled. Even then, the Gewisse were trying to claim land on the eastern borders and the Dumnonian lords there were willing to pay good wages for fighters of Caradoc's standing. The young Gwentman cast aside his plans for Gaul in favour of more immediate prospects at hand. He fought in many small skirmishes along the borders and earned a good reputation.

His story about his treacherous brother brought him much sympathy and he made great efforts to be noble in spirit in order to convince people he was a good and honest person. His present followers had absolutely no doubt about his sincerity and he drew great comfort from their support.

With a firm resolve that the four Saxon fugitives would not return home with twisted stories, he stood up, wrapped his cloak about himself and began to stroll along the scarp of the hill until he came to four of his men around a small campfire. Three were asleep behind the shelter of a windbreak made out of various scraps of animal hide.

The fourth man looked up at the sound of footsteps as Caradoc entered the lighted clearing. Recognising the young man as the one who'd been questioning him earlier in the day, he asked, "Have you been making your rounds of the lookouts?"

"Yes, my Lord. All the men are at their posts, keeping as good a watch as can be expected in the darkness."

"Anything unusual to report?"

"No, my Lord, all is quiet."

Caradoc nodded, staring into the flames, crouching down and holding out his hands to the warmth.

The youth looked at him hesitantly before venturing to say, "No sign of the reinforcements tonight."

Caradoc permitted himself a small smile, aware of the worry on the young man's mind. "Of course not," he said, "otherwise, you would have reported it to me."

There was a touch of reprimand in the reply, but the youth knew it was not the topic of conversation Caradoc objected to, but the way in which he'd tried to introduce the subject.

"Yes, my Lord, but I wondered whether perhaps the two men you sent out might have encountered Saxons." He grinned at Caradoc, knowing here was a man who preferred people to be direct and to the point when talking.

Raising an eyebrow, Caradoc said humorously, "It was a very weak way of trying to draw me into a conversation to allay your personal fears."

"Fears, my Lord?"

"Yes, fears—and do not be ashamed of the word. The only men who do not fear are either liars or fools." The lad smiled sheepishly and Caradoc went on: "We shall see more of our men tomorrow and our task here will be completed by the late morning, for better or worse. There is absolutely nothing to worry about." He gazed pensively into the night sky, and asked, "When do you go on your next inspection of the lookouts?"

"Soon, my Lord."

"You get some rest while I attend to that chore." Caradoc then got up and walked into the blackness, his sense of direction leading him towards the river, where there were three different lookout positions to be checked.

CHAPTER TWENTY

Incredibly, as far as the Saxons were concerned, the coracles did not overturn and they were able to cover a good distance in the dark, stopping well before daylight. Aldred had begun to suspect they were drawing near the river's end, where it opened out into the sea. The water was a little rougher now and although they could not see very far, they sensed the banks were becoming further apart.

When they'd landed on the eastern bank as quietly as possible, Aldred called them together to discuss the next part of their plan.

"We have certainly done well up to now," he began, "so I say we should continue along this bank while it is still dark. We must push on with the advantage we have gained on our enemy. I feel sure we are close to the sea. If we persevere through the night, we'll be walking along the shore by morning."

Sighelme agreed. "To stop now would be foolish and I think it would be a good idea to bring the coracles with us, too."

Ascertaining that Wilfred felt up to the walking, they were soon on their way. Aldred took the lead, carrying one of the coracles upon his back, Sighelme following with the other. Then came Wilfred, still feeling the strain in his leg muscles, while Cuthbert brought up the rear with sword drawn and shield at the ready to defend them at a moment's notice.

No one talked for fear of the sound carrying across the moors, inviting their hidden foes to come and seek them out.

The river sounded as if it was getting wider and they could smell the sea. They strained their ears, hoping to hear the sound of waves crashing against the rocks or a cliff face, but the river killed any such noise.

At last, just before daybreak, they could hear it; another milestone behind them, and they all felt elated.

"We don't need these coracles anymore—I certainly would not trust their buoyancy in the sea, would you?" asked Sighelme lightly.

"No, I would not," agreed Aldred with a smile. "We should hide them well though, in case the enemy find them and pick up our trail again."

Ripping the hides from the coracles to use for warmth at night, they cast the skeletons of the boats into the river and then resumed their journey.

It was Wilfred who drew their attention to the sea. "Look." He spoke in a whisper, yet forcefully, so they would note the excitement in his voice.

They all stopped and peered down the river through the mist.

"Woden be praised!" exclaimed Aldred. "Come on, let's get closer!"

"Wait," urged Cuthbert. The sound of galloping could be heard approaching.

"Two riders coming this way," said Sighelme. "Quick, into the river."

Wilfred had managed to clamber down the bank and splash knee-deep into the water, when he heard Cuthbert shout, "They've seen us—here they come!"

Aldred and Sighelme drew their swords in readiness.

Rounding the bend, the two horsemen were astonished to see the four Saxons, whom they recognised instantly. The Dumnonians were Caradoc's lookouts, posted not at the river to look for the Saxons, but in the moors, keeping a watch for Gryffith. They were hurrying now because Gryffith and a sizable force had been seen approaching their position, presumably to kill the Gwentman. Leaping onto their ponies, the warriors galloped towards the riverbank, choosing its flatter route in preference to the rough terrain of the moors.

Now Aldred ran halfway up the side of the hill and stopped to draw his sword, as did Cuthbert, and Sighelme shouted for Wilfred's spear, which the youngster obligingly threw to him.

One of the two horsemen veered off up the side of the hill towards the two Saxons, putting up his shield as Sighelme prepared to throw his spear. But the Saxon knew the horse was a better target than the rider and with all his bodily might, he launched the spear at the galloping pony and ran up the hill almost into the path of the second charger, who Cuthbert tackled by attacking the horse's leg with his sword. Both animals sprawled to the ground, tumbling their riders roughly onto the turf. One man jumped up straight away with his sword drawn and ready.

Aldred came forward, striking a blow at the side of the Dumnonian, who had lost his shield in the fall. With as much force as he could muster, the Celt smashed his fist into Aldred's face, knocking him off his feet and sending him rolling down the hill. Landing on the muddy pathway of the hill, Aldred was dazed, but Cuthbert saw the Dumnonian stride down towards him, with his sword clasped firmly in both hands.

"Aldred, look out!" yelled Cuthbert urgently, springing up and running towards the Dumnonian.

As the screaming Saxon approached, the Dumnonian turned to face him. With the grace and ease of a seasoned fighter, he successfully deflected Cuthbert's blow and tripped him up as he passed by. With vicious efficiency, he then brought his sword down forcefully, smashing through Cuthbert's skull.

Then he turned about to face Sighelme. The ginger head was soaking wet, but despite his pathetic-looking condition, the Dumnonian eyed him warily. Sighelme stood gazing at him, waiting for him to make the first move.

A scream from a man in his death throes suddenly came from behind Sighelme, startling the Dumnonian, whose eyes widened with fear as he saw his companion writhing on the ground with a spear pinning him to the earth. At the other end of the pole, Wilfred's hands were firmly clasped, as with gritted teeth, he pushed harder.

Realising he would soon be facing two opponents—three, even, if the chieftain recovered from the punch—the Dumnonian lunged at Sighelme's right side, but the Saxon's shield was up to block him.

Before Sighelme could launch a counterblow, the Dumnonian spun round on the spot, bringing his blade in for an attack on Sighelme's left side, which the young Saxon managed to avoid by jumping backwards and drawing in his stomach. The blade swished through the air, dangerously close.

As Sighelme struggled to regain his footing, his opponent's sword came down towards his head, striking the metal boss of his shield with a ringing sound and splintering the wood—almost shattering it. Lunging forward with his sword, Sighelme hoped to feel it penetrate his enemy, but no such thing: he'd have been slain were it not for Wilfred screaming a battle cry at the Dumnonian, forcing him to spin round to defend himself.

Wilfred had been sneaking up behind the Dumnonian, but was forced to reveal himself when he saw Sighelme about to be slain. Now the Celt swiped at him and Wilfred crouched low as the blade swept past the top of his head. From his painful, crouched position, he managed to thrust his spear forward, stabbing the Dumnonian in the thigh. As he yanked the spear back, the Celt roared with pain, for it was barbed. Wilfred began to pull harder, but then jumped clear as his opponent raised his sword over him.

"Stand clear, Wilfred." The words were incomprehensible to the Dumnonian, who spun round to see Sighelme, squaring up to him. With a loud cry of rage, the Dumnonian raised his sword and brought it down on the spear stuck in his leg, smashing it just above the head.

Sighelme, who was about to attack, refrained from doing so for the angry glare in the Dumnonian's eyes frightened him. Sensing this, the other man seized his opportunity to escape, stumbling and hopping to the riverbank, where he dived in and began to swim for his life.

"He's getting away!" yelled Sighelme. "Don't let him escape!" Casting aside his shield and sword, he ran down the hill and dived in the river in pursuit.

"Sighelme, wait," shouted Wilfred, hobbling awkwardly after him.

The Dumnonian stopped to look back and saw Sighelme swimming towards him, followed by Wilfred, who was obviously having difficulty in the water. Sighelme, however, was fit and the Dumnonian knew he could not outswim the ginger-headed Saxon. If he was to get away, he'd have to kill the heathen foe.

Seeing the Celt do a surface dive, Sighelme guessed his intention immediately and stopped swimming to tread water while unsheathing his scarmasax. Taking a deep breath, he, too, surface dived and swam under water, gripping the weapon between his teeth while he searched for the man.

All at once, they clashed, the Dumnonian grabbing Sighelme's wrist, stopping his intended thrust and the Saxon did the same in return. They twisted and turned together until both were forced to fight for the surface, continuing the struggle as they rose, each battling for a place at the top in order to take in air quickly and come down again before his opponent could fill his lungs.

Wilfred saw them burst out of the water as he tried, with difficulty, to swim to Sighelme's aid, but they were gone before he could swim another stroke.

Back in the depths, a thick red cloud of blood from the Dumnonian's injured leg spread around them. As the two warriors entwined their legs together, Sighelme suddenly thrust his head forward, trying to sink his teeth into the Dumnonian's throat. He was partially successful, for although he was unable to do precisely that, the force of his nose hitting the Dumnonian's larynx caused the man to release his breath in a rush of air and he kicked and thrashed out in panic. Desperately, violently, the Dumnonian made for the surface, swallowing and choking water all the way. He broke the surface, coughing and spluttering and before he could even begin to regain his breath, Sighelme emerged silently and gracefully, directly behind him.

It was all over with one quick cut of Sighelme's scarmasax, but he had no time to feel relief for a frantic call for help came from further down the river: the current was carrying Wilfred away. The youngster could not swim far with damaged ligaments and a cramp had caused him to stop swimming. He was battling to stay afloat. Sighelme immediately struck out towards him.

Aldred, gathering his concussed wit, was aware Sighelme and Wilfred had jumped into the water and now he managed to haul himself up onto his feet, despite being dazed. His head was throbbing and he felt sure his nose was broken, because sharp pains sent shock waves into his cheeks when he put his hand upon it. Looking around, all he could see was the Dumnonian that Wilfred had killed.

"Cuthbert, what of Cuthbert?" he wondered, then turned to see his blood-soaked body lying a little way up the hill. "Oh, no," he muttered.

Scrambling up the hill towards Cuthbert, all his wits were suddenly restored to him with the shocking realisation that another of his friends was dead and when he reached the spot, he fell to his knees. Cuthbert had been the one person with whom Aldred could communicate deeply—the friendship between the two had always been strong. Only moments before, they had been rejoicing the first sighting of the sea and now, that joy was shattered.

He knew he must put such thoughts behind him, for as chieftain, he still had the responsibility of Sighelme and Wilfred. It felt wrong to leave Cuthbert's corpse upon a hillside without ceremony and lamentation: but Rhinehold and Turnstan had had to be abandoned in the same way.

Standing up, he looked along the river to where Sighelme was trying to keep Wilfred above the water. Trying to cast aside thoughts of Cuthbert, he set off, distraught, along the riverbank to help them.

Wilfred and Sighelme were unaware he was coming, for all their efforts were devoted to staying afloat. With great difficulty, an exhausted Sighelme managed to bring Wilfred ashore, coughing and choking. He supported the youth a few steps from the bank before helping him to lie upon the turf. Both were cold and wet, but paid little heed to the discomfort.

"I must go back and get Aldred while you wait here—do you understand, Wilfred?" asked Sighelme. He nodded miserably and watched as Sighelme began to walk back along the riverbank. He had only walked a couple of paces when suddenly, an arrow swished through the air, straight at Sighelme's stomach.

He groaned between clenched teeth and turned to Wilfred as though he was about to run to him. Three more whistles, three more thuds. Sighelme arched his back, dropped to his knees, then fell flat on the ground, three arrows penetrating deep into his back.

Stunned, panic-stricken, Wilfred began to crawl towards him, calling his name.

Further up the hill, two of Sighelme's killers had restrung their bows and now had Wilfred firmly in their sights, but Caradoc called, "I want him alive!"

Three more warriors descended the hill and grabbed Wilfred's arms. The young Saxon made no protest as he allowed himself to be dragged off and brought before Caradoc, who was sitting upon his horse.

"Where are the other two?" asked Caradoc. The ensuing conversation, in Gaelic, was quite incomprehensible to Wilfred. When the chieftain had stopped talking, his listening warrior turned to Wilfred and added in the Saxon's language, "Where are the other two?"

"Dead," replied Wilfred.

"Where?"

"One is lying a little downstream, the other died in the forest." He cursed himself immediately the words were spoken—for although he had tried to cover for Aldred by saying he died in the forest, he knew the chieftain would probably be discovered when the Dumnonians went to check for Cuthbert's body.

The Dumnonian translated Wilfred's reply to Caradoc, whereupon the Gwentman immediately sent three of his riders to verify the story.

Wilfred's hands were tied together and he was leashed to one of the horsemen. The Dumnonians then set off in the direction of the beach with their demoralised, defeated Saxon prisoner.

CHAPTER TWENTY-ONE

Hearing the horsemen sent by Caradoc long before they came into view, Aldred jumped knee-deep into the shallow end of the river and crouched among the reeds, where he watched calmly as the three rode by. When they were safely out of sight, he clambered out of his hiding place to continue along the bank in search of Wilfred and Sighelme. He knew their presence was no longer a secret—or would not be for long—especially when the riders discovered the corpses of Cuthbert and the Dumnonian. If Wilfred and Sighelme were to have any chance of escaping, he must find them quickly.

But soon his hopes were shattered when he came upon Sighelme lying dead on the pathway. Climbing the hill, he expected to find Wilfred's corpse at the top and was surprised to see no sign of him.

Far away on the beach, a movement caught his eye. It was a line of horsemen with a person walking behind. Aldred squinted to try and identify the man walking and recognised Wilfred. This was his last man and he had to be rescued. Aldred would never go home alone, leaving all his warriors behind.

He sat down for a moment, struggling to eliminate from his mind the enormity of what had happened, concentrating all his thoughts on how to help Wilfred escape. Suddenly, he recalled the three horsemen who had ridden past him while he hid in the reeds. They would be searching the area where Cuthbert and the Dumnonian lay.

Aldred set off back to the area of the recent fight; he had no set plan, but would assess the situation when he arrived. Instead of travelling along the riverbank, he walked along the hilltop. He felt more secure when he could see all around him.

At the scene, he peered down and saw one of the Dumnonians holding three ponies, whilst the other two men rummaged about. One of them, holding a bloodstained sword, had apparently just killed one of the injured ponies which was lying there, while the other searched Cuthbert's corpse.

Aldred surveyed the scene carefully: two men had their backs to him, and the third, holding the horses, had a spear lying on the ground nearby. There might be a chance of killing the horse-minder and one of the other men quickly before the unfortunate Celts could realise what was happening—although the third man would still have time to prepare for an attack.

The Saxon crept down a knoll, making hardly any noise at all, and he was downwind from the horses. Coming as close as he could undercover, he stood up and boldly walked the short distance left between him and the horse-minder. The casual way in which he strolled caused no panic among the ponies and so the unfortunate Dumnonian suspected nothing. With one swift cut, his scarmasax felled the Dumnonian and as he slid to the ground, hot blood pumped out the savage gash in his throat .

The Dumnonian searching Cuthbert turned just in time to see Aldred throwing a spear at him with all the strength he could muster. He let out a breath as the spear smashed into his rib cage. He lay there, groaning in his death throes, as the third man stood petrified before his determined assailant.

With his two colleagues lying dead, the third Dumnonian, eyes wide with fear, drew his sword, watching the Saxon warily.

For some time, the men exchanged blows, which were always deflected by their shields. Back and forth they went along the riverbank, twisting and turning, sidestepping and blocking in a desperate duel to the sound of metal on metal and splintering wood. Soon, it became apparent the Dumnonian was tiring, allowing the determined Aldred to take the more aggressive role, while the Celt was forced to defend himself against the blows as best he could—and he performed this task admirably, even managing the odd unexpected thrust now and again. But Aldred was always ready for these little outbursts and as the

Dumnonian made a chance stab, he jumped sideways, allowing the blade to go harmlessly by. The Saxon then swung his blade at the man's unprotected right side and he crumpled to the ground, almost cut in half, but still alive and groaning.

Aldred struck again and again and soon, the hacked Celt lay silent. With a brief thought of respect for the dead man, Aldred then turned to the horses. Before mounting one, he picked up a discarded spear from amongst the litter of weapons lying around.

As he clambered onto the horse, the other two bolted away, but he paid them no heed, rather dug his heels into his own mount, causing the animal to speed off along the riverbank, back the way they had both originally come.

His adrenalin was pumping, firing him to confront the Dumnonians who had abducted Wilfred. As he rode over the last few hills before he came down upon the golden sands of the beach, he had no fear of the task ahead, for he knew exactly what he was going to do.

***

Caradoc had been waiting on the beach for his men to return, but unbeknown to him, all had perished, save those who were with him on the beach. He watched as the lone Saxon horseman galloped along the shoreline and came to a halt some distance away and began to shout out to the Celts in his own language.

"A challenge for Caradoc, if he is man enough to face me. I am Aldred, chieftain of this clan and wish for the chance to save my last kinsman."

"What is he saying?" asked Caradoc of the man who had translated for him when questioning Wilfred.

"He is saying he wishes to challenge you, the chieftain, in a straight and honourable duel, for he is the chieftain of the clan you have been hunting. Since you have killed all his men except the one prisoner you have with you, he is now in a position of dishonor; he still lives while his men are gone. If he wins his duel against you, he wants the prisoner to be set free, leaving us to take our revenge on himself."

"What if I win the duel?" asked Caradoc.

"You kill the Saxon chieftain and keep the prisoner, to do with as you will."

"Tell him I accept his challenge."

His men immediately began to protest, pointing out that the Saxon chieftain could be slain now anyway, but Caradoc would not listen to them. This was a noble man who challenged him and the Gwentman felt he, too, should act nobly by accepting. It was, after all, a show for his men. He had complete confidence that his skill at arms would be better than those of the young Saxon.

Aldred sat watching the Dumnonians, the tide foaming around his horse's feet as he awaited a reply to his challenge. It soon came. A middle-aged man of about thirty mounted his horse and walked it down to the shoreline a little distance from the Saxon.

"I, Caradoc of Gwent, accept your challenge, Saxon," he called.

Aldred did not understand the language: only the word 'Caradoc' meant anything to him and for a moment, he was confused. Pointing a finger at the Gwentman, he asked, "You are Caradoc?"

The Celt smiled at him and nodded his head in reply to what he thought the Saxon had asked.

Aldred's eyes lit up with excitement. Holding his spear in the air, he screamed jubilantly, dug his right heel into his mount's flank and turned the pony around to trot a little way back along the shoreline before turning to face Caradoc again.

A grim silence hung in the air, the only sound being the waves washing gently up on the beach.

Caradoc's men watched tensely for the Saxon to charge, while Wilfred's eyes were on the Gwentman. Suddenly, Aldred let out a loud battle cry as his horse surged forward and Caradoc calmly kicked his own into action as well.

Both warriors lowered their spears as they thundered towards each other, each looking along the pole, trying to fix the spearhead at a good angle to hit his opponent.

Swiftly, they closed on one another and as their mounts' hooves rose to a crescendo of thunder, contact was made with a loud clash. Aldred was smashed from his mount's back as the loud crack of Caradoc's broken spear filled the air. The Saxon splashed down into the water.

As the wave receded briefly from the shore, he could be seen twisting and turning in agony like a skewered fish. Caradoc's spear had penetrated deeply and broken off inside him. Finally, he stopped twisting and went rigid, trying to fight the pain. Slowly, he rose onto his knees as another wave came in, almost knocking him over. He looked up to see Caradoc dismounting, while two of his men ran up to join him. Blood oozed from the young chieftain's mouth as he tried desperately to compose himself and not bring dishonor upon his clan to the enemy before him.

Caradoc turned to speak to one of them, who looked at Aldred and said, "Your friend, whom we have as prisoner, will be set free."

Aldred nodded his head at Caradoc and smiled gratefully. Caradoc acknowledged this, before nodding sorrowfully at his two men to relieve the Saxon chieftain of his misery. The two Dumnonians strung arrows, lifted their bows, aimed, and released the shafts into the dying Saxon's breast. Aldred slumped backwards with his feet tucked under him. Another wave rolled him over face down into the wet, bloodstained sand.

Caradoc rode back to the rest of his men and told them to mount up. The Gwentman intended to go to the spot the prisoner had told him about, where he expected to find his three men, for better or worse. Before setting off, he had Wilfred set free and the young Saxon immediately ran towards the sea where Aldred lay.

***

As the Dumnonians headed off into the hills, Wilfred dragged his chieftain's corpse onto dry sand, but then he realised to bury him on the beach would not do; neither would the moors. It was then that the tranquil beauty of the sea impressed itself upon him and he decided it would be a perfect burial place for his chieftain.

He hoisted Aldred over his shoulder, staining his garments with blood, and carried him into the sea. When the water came up to Wilfred's chest, he released Aldred into the sea, pushing him gently away to be taken by the current.

"Oh, Woden," whispered the young warrior, "take my brave Lord unto your domain, let him feast with you and the other gods in Valhalla."

Wilfred then waded back to the shore, determined to find the dead bodies of Sighelme and Cuthbert in order to perform the same service for them.

CHAPTER TWENTY-TWO

Caradoc, intending to cut across the hills to the river instead of following the shoreline as Wilfred had done, never reached his destination. In the depths of a valley, he and his party were ambushed by Gryffith's considerably larger force.

Arrows rained down upon them from all sides. Horses went down, throwing their riders onto the turf. Caradoc's men ran around in confusion, only to be hit by arrows in whatever direction they ran.

The Gwentman lay face down on the ground with two arrows buried deep in his back. His horse was lying dead close by. With difficulty, Caradoc lifted his head and saw the youngster he had told not to worry about Gryffith. The young man had an arrow in his chest, but was still alive.

All around him, Caradoc could hear hooves stamping on the turf and he turned to face those nearest him.

Surrounded by many of his men, Gryffith peered down at him. An arrogant click of his fingers had two horses brought to the forefront of the group, corpses slung across their backs. These lifeless bodies were tumbled to the ground where they smacked to the earth like logs, stiff with rigor mortis.

Caradoc recognised them as the two messengers he had sent back for reinforcements when they had emerged from the forest and split up from Gryffith. He looked towards the wounded young man lying near to him, "I told you only fools do not fear. Well, I am a fool," he said forlornly.

"No, Lord Caradoc, not you—never," came the youngster's reply.

These words were the last thing Caradoc heard and they were more beautiful, more touching than anything he had heard in his life.

CHAPTER TWENTY-THREE

Wilfred went quietly, methodically, about his task of collecting the bodies of Sighelme and Cuthbert. Fortunately, his path never crossed with Gryffith and his men.

First, he carried Sighelme to the beach, then went back for Cuthbert, arming himself with the Celtic weapons lying about at his disposal. He had no desire for the Saxon weapons: they had belonged to his companions. Aldred and Sighelme had been cast afloat in the sea with swords sheathed, and he would do the same for Cuthbert.

His task complete, he continued to walk eastwards, following the coastline. Sometimes, he walked on the beach, others, along cliff tops. His progress was slow, for his legs still ached, but he plodded doggedly onwards, wishing only to return to the land of the West Saxons; back to his own hamlet.

Aldred, Sighelme, Cuthbert, Rhinehold, Turnstan and all those of the clan who had died during the fatal invasion of Dumnonia, had kin who would be deeply grieved by their deaths. All the able-bodied men of the hamlet were dead, except Wilfred, and now his people would be vulnerable to their feudal neighbours. The hamlet's chances of survival were nil; yet still Wilfred was determined to return.

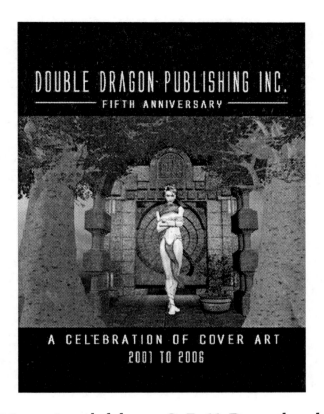